Lucinda knew Rockingham's reputation. But nothing had prepared her for the sight of him when he came into his drawing room.

His thick black hair was tousled, he was unshaven, and his tall athletic body was wrapped in an oriental dressing gown, gaudily embroidered to the point of decadence. His bare feet were thrust into Turkish slippers. His green eyes were bloodshot. A long night's gaming and drinking had worked its usual ruin. He had had only a bare two hour's sleep.

"Well?" he demanded.

"I have made a mistake," she said.

"Don't be silly," he snapped. "You have roused me at this unearthly hour, you have risked ruining your reputation, so you had better tell me what it's all about."

"I came here," Lucinda was forced to admit, "to ask you to marry me . . ."

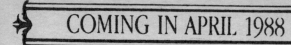

Marion Chesney

The Savage Marquess

A SIGNET BOOK

NEW AMERICAN LIBRARY

NAL BOOKS ARE AVAILABLE AT QUANTITY DISCOUNTS WHEN USED TO
PROMOTE PRODUCTS OR SERVICES. FOR INFORMATION, PLEASE WRITE TO
PREMIUM MARKETING DIVISION, NEW AMERICAN LIBRARY,
1633 BROADWAY, NEW YORK, NEW YORK 10019.

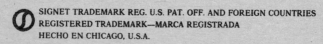

SIGNET, SIGNET CLASSIC, MENTOR, ONYX, PLUME, MERIDIAN and
NAL BOOKS are published by NAL PENGUIN INC.,
1633 Broadway, New York, New York 10019

First Printing, March, 1988

1 2 3 4 5 6 7 8 9

PRINTED IN THE UNITED STATES OF AMERICA

For Tilda Chesney Grenier, with love

1

"My dear, he's back! Rockingham's back!"

The Earl of Clifton sighed noisily and rustled his newspaper defensively. He had brought his wife to London to prepare for their daughter, Ismene's coming-out. He had wrenched himself away from his beloved country home for the few months of the Season and felt he had done enough.

"Who is Rockingham?" he asked testily.

The Countess of Clifton sat down in a flurry of satin and lace. "You are indeed out of the world," she said with that affected laugh of hers which never failed to grate on the earl's nerves. "The Marquess of Rockingham. The Savage Marquess. The one they say has sold his soul to the devil. He disappeared for years after that scandal when his mistress tried to hang herself. Now he is back and announces he is looking for a wife."

"Rich?" asked the earl, trying to show some interest.

"Vastly so. And devilishly handsome."

"Then he should have little trouble in finding one." The earl yawned and picked up his newspaper again.

"But that is the point! No lady of breeding could face the idea of such a monster. 'Tis said he beats his servants."

"Stout fellow," came the languid voice of her spouse from behind his newspaper barrier. "Some of 'em could do with a beating."

"And he gambles and drinks to excess."

"Then he won't stay rich for long."

"Ah, but that is why they say he has sold his soul to the devil, for he mostly wins."

"Then if he is such a nasty character," said the earl in an abstracted voice, "he probably cheats. Since he is obviously not a suitable prospect for Ismene, may we drop this tedious subject?"

Lady Clifton pouted. She had once been a great beauty and still adopted all the mannerisms of a youthful belle. "You take no interest in Ismene's welfare," she said. "You know Ismene is monstrous lonesome in London and craves company of her own age. You promised and promised to find her a companion and yet you do nothing about it."

"I had hoped," said Lord Clifton, putting down his newspaper with an air of defeat, "that our daughter might have managed to endear herself to some members of her own sex. It seems hard I should have to pay for a companion as well as paying the expenses of a Season."

"But don't you see! It is because Ismene is so very beautiful. All are jealous of her."

At that moment Lady Ismene flounced into the room. She was indeed a dazzling beauty, from her pomaded brown curls to her little rosebud mouth and dainty figure.

"What are you talking about?" she asked.

"I was trying to interest your father in Rockingham's return."

"La! No one talks of anything else. I confess I am bored with the Savage Marquess before I even set eyes on the man. I asked that cat, Miss Sommers, to go driving in the park with me and she said she was too busy. And yet I have just seen her driving in a vis-à-vis with that antidote, Miss Flanders."

"Perhaps she had a previous arrangement," said the countess. "We have also been discussing the idea of hiring a companion for you."

"That would be fun," said Ismene, pleating the fringe of her stole. "I mean, a companion would have to go everywhere with me, would she not?"

"Your father has promised to attend to the matter urgently. Whom are you going to employ, Clifton?"

The earl threw down his newspaper and

marched to the door. "I am going to my study to think about it," he snapped.

Once in his study, the earl sighed with relief and sent for brandy to soothe his nerves. This Marquess of Rockingham would never put up with such henpecking, he thought. But, he decided, the sooner he found someone to accompany Ismene, then the sooner he would be left in peace.

He went over to his desk, dipped a pen in the standish, and furrowed his brow as he turned over the names of various poor relations. If only he could think of someone staid and practical who would be a good influence on his spoilt daughter.

His thoughts turned longingly to his country home, Beechings. In his mind's eye he could see the graceful porticoed entrance, the rose gardens, and the smooth lawns. On the edge of his estates lay the village of Sarral, a pretty, picturesque place with its old Norman church.

As a picture of the church floated across his inner eye, he sat upright. What had been the name of that curate? Westerville, that was it. He had read a most affecting sermon one Christmas when the vicar had been ill. Sterling fellow. And he had a daughter who must now be Ismene's age!

He had heard Westerville was ill. Now, in

return for the use of his daughter, he would send this Westerville the best physician and enough funds to ensure he could hire proper care while his daughter was in London. What was the girl's name? Pretty thing. Lovely hair. Ah, Lucinda, that was it.

The Earl of Clifton began to write busily.

Lucinda Westerville sat in the shed in the garden of her family cottage, waiting for the water in the copper to boil. The vast copper basin held by its brick framework had been laboriously filled with pails and pails of water, carried from the pump. In a basket on the floor beside the copper lay a pile of sheets. Once the water was boiling, Lucinda would put them in the copper, boil them for an hour, and hope that some of their yellowish hue would be miraculously taken out. The women in the village used a mixture of chicken dung to whiten yellowing linen, but Lucinda could not bring herself to mix anything so evil-smelling into the wash.

Lucinda was not pretty by the standards of London fashion. Her nose was too short and her mouth was a trifle too generous. Her eyes were hazel and fringed with long lashes and her chestnut hair was thick and had a natural curl. But she was too tall and too thin in an age when plump bosoms and rounded arms were much admired.

The water in the copper began to bubble. She raised the heavy wooden lid and then heaved up the basket of soiled linen and tipped in the contents.

She went out into the garden, preparatory to going into the house to make a nourishing vegetable broth for her sick father.

The spring sunlight struck down on her bare head and a light warm breeze flirted with the darned skirts of her muslin gown. She turned away from the house instead and wandered down to the end of the garden, where there was a rustic seat under the spreading branches of an apple tree.

She wanted to pray for her father's recovery, but found she could not. What kind of God was up there who could ensure that the vicar, the Reverend Mr. Glossop, his wife, and two nasty daughters continued to live in riches and health while her father wasted away? When his curate, Mr. Westerville, had first fallen ill, Mr. Glossop had cut his miserable wages in half and had considered he was doing a great Christian act by paying him even a pittance. Lucinda knew it would be only a matter of time before Mr. Glossop ceased to pay him anything at all.

She had even humbled herself by going to

ask Mrs. Glossop for work, but that sour and snobbish lady had remarked acidly that Lucinda's place was at her father's bedside. In vain did Lucinda plead they had not enough money to buy medicine. Mrs. Glossop had ceased to listen and her two daughters had cast sly, pitying smiles in Lucinda's direction and had continued to play with their latest expensive toy, a clockwork nightingale.

There seemed to be no way she could earn money. A month ago, Tom Barnet, the squire's son, had called and had begged her to marry him. He was a tall, gawky youth, quite stupid, and given to long drinking bouts. Lucinda had told him gently she would think it over. By the end of the day, she had decided to accept. Her marriage to the squire's son would ensure expert nursing and medicine for her father.

But Tom Barnet did not call again. She had just been summoning up her courage to call at his home when she learned from Mrs. Glossop that Tom had been sent away on the Grand Tour "because it is rumored he has fallen for some undesirable village girl."

The post boy's horn, sounding from the front of the cottage, broke into her bitter thoughts. She ran through the garden and along the side of the cottage to the front.

"Letter for Mr. Westerville," said the post boy. "Got a crest and all."

Lucinda took the letter from him and examined the heavy-crested seal. She recognized the Earl of Clifton's coat of arms.

She went indoors and carried the letter upstairs to her father's bedroom.

Mr. Westerville was lying in an old four-poster bed. A shaft of sunlight fell on his thin, wasted face. His sparse gray locks straggled down on his shoulders.

He opened his eyes as Lucinda came into the bedroom, and gave her a faint, sweet smile.

"Was that the post boy?"

"Yes, Papa. A letter for you with the Earl of Clifton's crest."

"Then it is good news," said Mr. Westerville, a faint tinge of pink staining his cheeks.

"Good news!" cried Lucinda. "Oh, Papa, I know what it is. You have written to the earl for help."

"Not I."

"Then how can you possibly know it is good news?"

"I have prayed for assistance," said the curate with simple dignity. "I have been daily awaiting an answer to my prayers. I do not care for myself, but I care very deeply about your future, Lucinda."

"It is your health that matters," Lucinda said passionately. "I can look after myself."

"Raise me up," said Mr. Westerville, "and bring me my glass and we shall see what the earl has to say."

Lucinda helped him to sit up against the pillows and then handed him a large magnifying glass. He fumbled for a long time with the seal before he got the letter open. But Lucinda was no longer excited about the possible contents of the letter. She was sure it contained some trivial request. She envied her father his simple faith but could not share it.

Mr. Westerville read the letter very carefully and then put it down on the worn quilt and looked up at his daughter with tears in his eyes. "God is good," he said.

"I hope He has seen fit to send us some money," said Lucinda tartly.

"Better than that," said Mr. Westerville. "The earl wishes you to travel to London to be a companion to the Lady Ismene. No!" He raised a thin, transparent hand to check the outburst he saw on Lucinda's lips. "I shall not be left uncared for. I am to be taken to Beechings, the earl's home, during your absence and there attended by a London physician and given all care and comfort."

Lucinda began to tremble. "You are sure? Oh, do let me see the letter, Papa."

He handed it to her, closed his eyes, and moved his lips in prayer.

Lucinda scanned the contents quickly. It was indeed as her father had said, but there was more detail. The earl wished Lucinda to travel to London almost immediately and was sending his coach, which should arrive a week following the letter. During that week, his servants would move Mr. Westerville to Beechings.

"A week!" said Lucinda. "What about clothes? I have nothing grand enough for London."

Her father stopped praying and opened his eyes. "I have no doubt they will furnish you with a wardrobe as befits your position. I have no more worries now."

Lucinda leaned forward and kissed his cheek. "So why do you still pray?" she teased.

"I gave thanks," said Mr. Westerville, "and then asked that you should be wed to a man worthy of you."

"Prayers are not always answered," Lucinda said.

"Yes, they are," sighed Mr. Westerville. "Always. Although sometimes the answer is no. But I am sure there is a gentleman waiting for you in London, a gentleman of refinement and breeding and infinite kindness. . . ."

"Why does no one answer this damned

bell," roared the Marquess of Rockingham. "Oh, a pox on my curst head!"

"The staff all gave notice this morning, my lord," said Chumley, his wooden-faced valet.

"What! Why? I pay them enough."

"Your lordship was in your altitudes when you returned from Watier's last night. You had unhitched one of your carriage horses and ridden it home, my lord."

"So what's the fuss?"

"Your lordship rode the animal in through the front door and up the staircase. The horse was unnerved and behaved accordingly. The resultant mess on the stairs gave the housekeeper the vapors. The housemaids went into hysterics. You dismounted and slapped two of them. You then collapsed on the landing and fell asleep. When two of the footmen lifted you up to carry you to bed, you awoke and attempted to throw one of them over the banisters. Before you left · for Watier's, you had a wild party here, attended by ladies of cracked reputation. I have this morning engaged two scrubbing women to clean up the worst of the mess, and after I have attended to your lordship, I shall call at an agency and employ more staff."

"Oh, the deuce. Since when were servants so nice in their tastes?"

"It is the changing fashion," said Chumley, stooping to pick up a soiled cravat. "I believe licentiousness and drunkenness are quite exploded."

The marquess, who had picked up a hand mirror to study his ravaged face, threw it furiously at his valet, who fielded it with the dexterity of long practice.

But as the valet handed the mirror back to his master and turned away, the very stiffness of his back registered disapproval.

"Oh, the deuce," said the marquess. "I didn't try to hit you. But you are too free-spoken, Chumley."

"I always have been," said Chumley. "It is the only way I can cope with your lordship's humors and stay in your employ."

"You would have humors too, you nut-cracker-faced martinet, if you drank as much as I. This little gathering I held here—very wild, was it?"

"The wildest, my lord."

"It's this damned ennui that plagues me. What a pesky, boring frivolity this London Season is."

"Then may I suggest, my lord, we resume our travels and adventures? You are not out of sorts when you are not bored."

"My adventures are over for the moment. I must find a wife."

"My lord!"

"It is not unusual. I want sons."

"Your lordship's reputation is such that I fear your lordship will have to learn to court the ladies."

"Fiddle! When did a rich and titled man have to court any of the creatures? Why, Lady Bessie Dunstable, the belle of two Seasons, has settled for that creaking old duke."

"The duke is tranquil and manageable. I fear rumor has it that you frighten the fair sex."

"Well, I shall behave prettily for just as long as it is necessary to find me a bride. Does that suit you?"

"Your liaison with Mrs. Deauville is well known, my lord. Mrs. Deauville is good *ton*. Society expects you to marry her sooner or later."

"Then society is quite mad. Maria Deauville amuses me, but she would not be faithful to me for a twelvemonth were she married to me."

Chumbley began to strop a razor. "Your lordship's cousin, the Honorable Zeus Carter, is waiting below."

"Why did you not tell me sooner? Not that I am interested in seeing the weakling."

"I feared the intelligence would put your lordship in a passion had I divulged it first thing this morning," said Chumley, advancing on his master with hot towels. "I can tell him you are not at home."

"No, I may as well see him. I wonder what brings him to London. His regiment is in Portugal."

The Honorable Zeus waited impatiently in the library downstairs. He had been a lusty baby, a fact that had prompted his doting parents to bless him with the name of Zeus. But he had grown up tall and weedy and effeminate. He was the marquess's heir. He paced up and down the library, occasionally pausing to narrow his eyes and imagine what the room would look like redecorated to his own taste. The way Rockingham was going on, he could not live very long.

He studied his rouged face in the glass over the fireplace. It was, he thought, twisting his head from side to side, an aristocratic and noble face, marked with faint lines of sensitivity. Such a face should not be exposed to the burning sun of the Peninsula, and such delicate shell-like ears should not be abused by the roar of cannon. He had sold out of his regiment. Now he was in need of funds. He had had to exit from his lodgings by the back door, as the duns were camped out at the front.

Goodness, this room was like a pigsty! One of Rockingham's notorious parties, no doubt. A red silk garter hung from the chandelier and a scanty lace shift was draped around a bust of Plato above the door. He wondered idly how it had got up there.

He rang the bell impatiently, but no one answered. He peered around the door into the shadowy hall and called, "Wine, I say! Where's the decanter?" But only silence answered his call. Rockingham's servants must have given notice, apart from that stiff martinet of a valet, who stuck by his master through thick and thin.

Mr. Carter slumped petulantly into a chair and closed his eyes. In no time at all, he was fast asleep.

After half an hour, he came slowly awake, sensing someone was looming over him. He opened his eyes wide, under short stubby lashes darkened with lampblack, and stared up.

The saturnine face of the Marquess of Rockingham looked down at him.

"Greetings, coz," said Mr. Carter, struggling upright. "How goes the world?"

"Tolerably well," said the marquess curtly. "What brings you here?"

"To make sure you are in good health."

The marquess looked at his cousin

cynically. He had odd green eyes, like the eyes of a cat. Apart from purplish bruises under those eyes, Mr. Carter noticed with a now-familiar twinge of disappointment that his cousin looked remarkably fit. His linen was impeccable, his tailoring excellent enough to make even Brummell envious, and his cravat was a miracle of starch and sculptured folds. His hair shone with all the healthy blue-black sheen of a male blackbird's plumage. His long, strong legs, encased in skintight pantaloons, owed nothing to padding or false calves. Mr. Carter looked sadly down at his own legs and then muttered under his breath. One of his false wooden calves had slipped. He petulantly jerked the harness that held it up under his stocking back into place.

"Well, as you can see, I am still alive, so take yourself off," said the marquess, breaking the silence. "Why aren't you with your regiment?"

"I sold out."

"Indeed!"

"I am not cut out for a soldier's life. The men were disgracefully undisciplined. When I shouted, 'Charge!' they paid no attention."

"You should have tried shouting your orders from the front of your troops and not the back," said the marquess nastily. "I suppose you are come to dun me."

Mr. Carter flushed. "You always credit me with the worst motives. I am come—"

"Stow it," said the marquess rudely. "How much?"

"Five thousand pounds," bleated Mr. Carter. He shrank back in his chair, prepared to endure the blast of his formidable cousin's wrath. The sum was actually two thousand and he hoped to placate the marquess by eventually seeming to settle for a lesser sum.

But to his surprise, the marquess strode over to his desk, sat down, and began to write.

"Do you mean you are going to lend me the money?" squeaked Mr. Carter.

"I am giving it to you, as you have no intention of paying it back. I may as well start off respectably married rather than having a cousin in the Fleet."

Sheer shock forced Mr. Carter to leap to his feet. "Married! You! Who is the lady?"

"I don't know," grumbled the marquess, busily writing. "Does it matter?"

Mr. Carter let out a slow breath. Perhaps all hope was not lost. He tittered nervously. "You cannot just get married like that."

"Oh, yes I can. I'll marry the first suitable female who'll have me. As long as she can breed, of course."

This was too much. Mr. Carter sank slowly back down into his chair, pulled a Chinese fan from his pocket, and began to fan himself vigorously.

"Children," he moaned.

"Lots and lots," said the marquess cheerfully, sanding the draft and holding it out. "Now, take this and run or I may change my mind."

Mr. Carter clutched the chair back for support as he stood up again. He took the draft in his little pink hands, delicately stained with cochineal.

Then he tucked it away in the tails of his bottle-green coat. "I say, coz, that means I won't be your heir."

"You never really were," said the marquess. "I always planned to marry before I reached my dotage."

"But you are already too old. You are thirty-five."

The marquess sighed. "Give me back that draft, Zeus."

"No need for that. My wretched tongue. Apologize most humbly."

"Then good-bye."

"I give you good day, coz." Mr. Carter made a magnificent leg, almost touching his kneecap with his nose and then straightening up with many flourishes of a heavily scented handkerchief.

A sudden pain stabbed behind the marquess's eye. He picked up the inkwell and threw it. Mr. Carter darted out and shut the door just as the heavy brass inkwell struck it.

He walked a little way away from the marquess's town house, his heart beating hard. He had been so sure the marquess would have killed himself on some of his adventures or have drunk himself to death. Marriage!

He could only hope that no woman would take the wicked marquess as husband.

2

As the Earl of Clifton's traveling carriage turned into Grosvenor Square, Lucinda began to feel sick with apprehension. So much depended on this post. It had been wonderful to see her father accommodated in a sunny room at Beechings and surrounded with every attention and comfort. She must do nothing to jeopardize this marvelous opportunity.

She must not let Mrs. Glossop's parting words sound in her ears—but sound they still did as the carriage rolled to a stop in front of an imposing mansion. "Ismene will soon send you packing," Mrs. Glossop had said. "She always was a spoilt, willful thing. You are a new toy, Lucinda, and she will soon tire of you."

Lucinda wearily climbed down from the carriage, feeling stiff and shaky after the journey. She was ushered into a large hall with a black-and-white-tiled floor by a stately butler. The butler in turn summoned the housekeeper, remarking that the family was not at home, and he did not know when they were due to return.

Following the housekeeper up the staircase, Lucinda could not help wishing that Ismene, who knew the hour of her arrival, had stayed to welcome her. The richness of the house was intimidating, as were the indifferent painted eyes of the rows of Clifton ancestors who stared down at this shabby interloper from their gold frames on either side of the staircase.

"I have given you the room next to Lady Ismene so you can be on call at all times," said the housekeeper. "My name is Mrs. Friend. Would you care for tea?"

"Yes, thank you," said Lucinda, untying the strings of her bonnet.

The housekeeper gave a slight bob. Lucinda did not merit a full curtsy. When she had left, Lucinda looked about her. It was a pleasant sunny room with a single bed covered with a chintz canopy. The furniture was somewhat shabby, as if it had been brought down from the attics for her use. But the towels by the toilet table were soft and white and the cakes of soap were delicately scented.

A scratching at the door was followed by the entrance of a housemaid in a print gown and muslin cap, followed by a footman carrying Lucinda's trunk. "I shall do my own unpacking," said Lucinda, pink staining her cheeks. She did not want these grand London servants to see how very few gowns she had.

She smiled gently but they returned her smile with blank stares. Lucinda was that most despicable of creatures in the servants' eyes—neither fish nor fowl, neither member of the family nor rich guest.

Lucinda slowly unpacked her clothes and put them away. Then she washed herself as thoroughly as she could and changed into a simple white cotton gown ornamented with little sprigs which she had embroidered herself. The cotton was a trifle coarse, but Lucinda was a good dressmaker, and she hoped its fashionable lines would make it acceptable to her new employer.

She pulled a battered chair over to the window, took a book from her reticule, and began to read. A footman brought in a tray with tea and biscuits. Lucinda had learned her lesson quickly. She neither smiled nor thanked him. Mrs. Glossop never thanked servants. It was not the Done Thing. Lucinda had assumed that was because of Mrs. Glossop's customary lack of good breeding, but her quick intelligence told her that she would fare better with these London servants if she maintained a chilly distance.

The tea was freshly made and the sweet biscuits an unaccustomed luxury. After she had finished, Lucinda resumed her reading. The window was open and the warm sunlight flooding the room began to make her feel sleepy.

Ismene walked into Lucinda's room an hour later and stood in the doorway surveying this new companion, who was fast asleep in the chair. Lucinda, Ismene noticed, was not precisely pretty, and that was good. Ismene would brook no competition from any companion. But the wealth of her chestnut hair with its glinting gold highlights made Ismene's eyes narrow. Ismene's own hair had to be rolled in curl papers every night. As if Ismene's hard stare had penetrated her dreams, Lucinda suddenly came awake. She blushed and stood up. "I am sorry, Lady Ismene," she said, immediately guessing this fashion plate must be her new mistress. "I was tired after the journey."

"No matter," said Ismene. She crossed to the large William and Mary wardrobe, pulled open the doors, and raised her thin eyebrows at the scanty array of frocks. "You are coming with me to Almack's tonight," she said. "You cannot wear any of these. Couldn't you have done better than this?"

"I have no money," said Lucinda.

"Oh, well, my maid, Kennedy, will make over one of mine for you. There's a yellow thing I'm tired of. You can have it. And your hair had better be cut."

"My hair!" Lucinda looked at Ismene in bewilderment. Lucinda's hair was her only vanity. "Why?"

"Why, *my lady*," corrected Ismene severely. "I don't like all that hair of yours and that's reason enough for you."

Lucinda thought wearily of her father. "Very well, my lady," she said quietly. "It shall be as you wish."

"Then we shall be friends!" cried Ismene with a sudden change of mood. "You may call me Ismene when we are not in company. See, I quite dote on you already. Now, come to my room and we shall talk to Kennedy."

She put an arm around Lucinda's waist and led her into her own bedroom, which was richly furnished. "Kennedy," she said to a lady's maid, "this is my new companion, Miss Westerville. You must be quick and make over one of my old ball gowns for her. The yellow, I think. A trifle unbecoming, but since Lucinda is only a companion and may not dance, it will not matter. Now, Lucinda, let me tell you all about my beau. He is Jamie Macdonald, a Scotch laird, not rich, of course

—the Scotch hardly ever are—but so divinely handsome and *quelles jambes*, my sweet, enough to make one swoon. He is not indifferent to me, I assure you, for he pressed my hand quite warmly when we met in the figure of the dance t'other night. Oh, he apologized and said he had momentarily lost his footing, but I knew better, and threw him a speaking glance. Of course, Mama noticed and said I must at all times remember what was due to our name. But it is quite the thing to have an inamorata after one is married, and Jamie Macdonald would do very well. I have it in me to inspire great passion."

"Indeed," said Lucinda politely, grimacing as she tried to stifle a yawn.

"I must be engaged before the Season is over. If one is not engaged, then one is counted a great failure. Of course, there is always the Savage Marquess. 'Tis said he will marry anyone, but who would dare? So wild and rude and violent! And he has a mistress in keeping, a Mrs. Deauville, who is not an opera dancer or a Cyprian, but a lady of the *ton*, and accepted most everywhere—except Almack's, of course."

"Who is this savage marquess?" asked Lucinda.

"Rockingham. He looks like the devil, it is said, but too devastatingly handsome for words." Ismene kissed the tips of her fingers.

"Is he rich?"

"Terribly so."

"Then surely he has only to snap his fingers." Lucinda looked surprised. Despite her poor circumstances, Lucinda was of good family, her father being the younger son of a baronet. She knew, from infrequent visits to her rich relations—relations who had failed to reply to any of her letters begging for help for her father—that the whole meaning of a fashionable marriage was business. Marriage was rightly regarded as a serious matter, with far more at stake than the gratification of momentary infatuations. Social compatibility, adequate provision for children and for the bride should she chance to become widowed, the formation of desirable connections, and the advancement of the family's standing were the important purposes served by matchmaking.

Only when an aristocrat had fallen on hard times and needed to save his lands did he look outside his own caste. It was often whispered that marriage with the daughters of the mercantile class had infused much-needed new blood into some ancient lines which had begun to show alarming signs of producing totty-headed eccentrics.

"Oh, ladies have fallen in love with him, or

so I hear, only to be shattered by his uncouth ways. It is rumored he is to attend the assembly rooms tonight. A situation *très piquant, n'est-ce pas*?"

"Quite."

"You must make sure he does not form a *tendre* for me. I should shake like a jelly with fear. We dine early. I suppose it is *comme il faut* for you to sit with us. It is not as if you are precisely a servant. Come along."

"I would appreciate an opportunity of trying this dress on Miss Westerville first, my lady," said Kennedy, shaking out the folds of a yellow ball gown.

"We haven't got the time, so you must guess your best," said Ismene airily. "Come, Lucinda."

Lucinda had never before hated anyone. She disliked Mrs. Glossop and her daughters, but tolerated them. One could not expect to like everyone. So Lucinda was quite surprised at the strength of her sudden savage dislike for her young employer. She thought Lady Ismene detestable: vain, silly, empty-headed, selfish, and cruel. She knew instinctively that Ismene would soon turn against her, the way a spoilt child will smash a doll. But somehow, she must try to last in her post as companion for as long as possible. Only when her father wrote to say he was returned to full health could she begin to relax.

The Countess of Clifton was much as Lucinda expected Ismene's mother to be—every bit as chattering and empty-headed as her daughter. The earl was silent and taciturn, but Lucinda sensed in him some strength of character.

"And you should see poor Lucinda's gowns!" cried Ismene as the dessert was brought in. "So countrified. Why, Mama, only see the texture of the cotton in that gown she has on. Quite peasant."

"Kennedy will no doubt run her up something for Almack's," said the countess, raising a quizzing glass and surveying Lucinda with a cold eye.

"Yes, that old yellow thing," said Ismene. She stared at the dessert, which was a miracle of the confectioner's art, a sugar lion crouched in a bed of sugarplums. She raised a silver knife and decapitated the lion with one quick stroke. Little puffs of sugar dust floated up into the sunbeams in the dining room.

"Now that you have ruined it, Ismene," said her father, speaking for the first time, "you may as well eat some of it."

"No," said Ismene with a shrug. "I don't want any." The earl's lips tightened but he said nothing. "So," went on Ismene, "it will not matter much what Lucinda looks like, for she will not be dancing."

"Why?" demanded the earl suddenly.

"Stupid. Companions don't dance."

"Yes, they do," said the earl firmly. "It will look most odd in you, Ismene, if you have a young companion who is not allowed to dance. In fact, it would be better to introduce Lucinda as your friend."

"Why, pray?"

"So that you do not continue to be the only young lady in London who appears to be incapable of making friends."

"Ismene would have scores of friends," said her mother loyally, "were she not so very pretty. They are all jealous."

"As you will," said the earl, appearing to lose interest.

"Of course," said Ismene slowly, "there may be something in what you say. But don't go giving yourself airs, Lucinda, or I shall be obliged to send you packing."

"You will send Lucinda packing when I say so and not before," said the earl.

"Pooh," retorted his wife. "If you are going to be unpleasant, Clifton, we may as well leave you to your port."

She picked up a little water bowl, filled her mouth with some of the liquid, gargled noisily, and spat the water back into the bowl. "Come, Lucinda," said the countess, dabbing her mouth with her napkin. "You will play for us before we retire to dress."

* * *

Ismene ordered Kennedy to see to the cutting of Lucinda's hair, and then became absorbed in her own preparations for the ball. Monsieur Roux himself, that famous hairdresser, was to arrange her own hair in one of the new fashionable styles. Kennedy was unimpressed by Monsieur Roux's reputation. He was a foreigner, a servant like herself. She met him in the corridor as he was leaving Ismene's bedroom after having done her hair. "Off so soon!" exclaimed Kennedy, seeing the hairdresser making for the stairs. "There is another lady to attend to. A Miss Westerville. You're to cut her hair." She held open the door of Lucinda's room. "In here," she said with an ungracious jerk of her head.

Monsieur Roux opened his mouth to say he would not do any more that evening, but then gave a resigned Gallic shrug. He was shrewd and clever and knew that the aristocracy might favor high-handed hairdressers for a short time, but that a man who was discreet, civil, and obliging would remain at the top of his profession for a long time.

Lucinda blushed as he came in, followed by Kennedy. She was attired only in her shift. But Kennedy seemed to find nothing amiss. "This is Monsoor Rooks," said Kennedy, "come to cut off your hair," and, with that, she exited with a loud slamming of the door to show both parties how low they ranked in her idea of precedence.

Monsieur Roux looked at the wealth of Lucinda's chestnut hair. "Short crops are highly fashionable," he said, "but with hair such as yours, Miss Westerville, surely it would be a crime to spoil such beauty."

"I am Lady Ismene's companion," said Lucinda in a colorless voice, "and her instructions are that my hair must be cut."

Monsieur Roux glanced quickly at her reflection in the mirror, his sharp black eyes noticing the compression of the soft mouth and the glitter of unshed tears in the large eyes.

"Very well," he said. He picked up his long, sharp scissors. Lucinda closed her eyes.

All at once she remembered her mother, dead these past six years, with ache and longing; her pretty, vivacious mother who made light of their poverty. Lucinda felt lost and alone in an alien world. Her throat ached with the effort of holding back her tears.

Monsieur Roux muttered something and then rang the bell. When a chambermaid answered it, he said, "Fetch my boy. You will find him waiting for me belowstairs. And tell him to bring my cases." Thinking his work completed for the evening, Monsieur Roux had sent his boy downstairs to wait for him.

He was all at once determined to create the most fashionable crop in London.

When the boy arrived, Monsieur Roux rapped out orders for pomades and lotions.

After some time, Kennedy came in with the yellow gown over her arm and stood waiting impatiently. "Are you going to take all night?" she demanded. "Lady Ismene does not like to be kept waiting."

"No," murmured the hairdresser, "I am just finished."

He stood back and admired his handiwork. "You may open your eyes now, Miss Westerville," he said.

But Lucinda did not look in the mirror. She got to her feet and turned to face Kennedy.

"You foreign rogue!" said Kennedy, her normally bad-tempered face cracking in a grin. "Off with you."

Kennedy deftly helped Lucinda into the gown, draped a shawl around her shoulders, handed her gloves and a fan, and told her to make haste. "But don't you want to see yourself?" said the lady's maid.

She pushed Lucinda toward the wardrobe and swung open one of the doors, which had a long mirror on the inside.

Lucinda looked amazed at the modish stranger facing her. The primrose-yellow gown was cleverly tucked to flatter her thin figure. Her head was a riot of curls, brushed and pomaded so that the gold threads in them shone in the candlelight.

"Make the most of it," said Kennedy sourly, "for the sight of you is going to put her ladyship in a passion. Here, give me that shawl. The night is sharp. Put on this cloak, see"— lifting a cloak of Lucinda's from the wardrobe —"and put the hood over your head, so she don't see what you look like or you'll never be allowed out of the house."

Too bewildered to protest, Lucinda did as she was bid.

Downstairs, Ismene berated her for taking so much time, but made no remark on Lucinda's cloaked and hooded appearance.

Ismene herself looked ravishing in a gown of gold net with gold and silver embroidery. Mindful of her duties, Lucinda told her so, and was rewarded with a complacent smile. "I feel we shall deal together tolerably well," said Ismene.

At Almack's, Kennedy deliberately saw to her mistress first so that Ismene and her mother had left the anteroom before Kennedy removed Lucinda's cloak.

Lucinda went shyly into the entrance hall and joined the Earl and Countess of Clifton and Ismene.

Ismene's eyes bulged. "You look a fright," she said crossly.

The earl put up his quizzing glass. "My dear Miss Westerville," he said, "you are so modish, so beautiful, that I could only wish your father were here to see you."

He walked ahead, and the countess and Ismene, darting furious glances at Lucinda, followed.

"What on earth was Roux about, to turn the companion into a fashion plate?" hissed the countess. "Kennedy was told to cut off Lucinda's hair."

"When malice is confounded, it is always upsetting," said the earl equably.

As they entered the ballroom, a roped-off square of floor rather like a ring at a cattle auction, Lucinda thought nervously it was as well she was only a companion with no expectations of social success. To arrive at Almack's as a Miss making her come-out must be even more terrifying. How hard everyone's eyes were! How assessing. How they did stare so!

Heads bent and voices whispered. Lucinda did not know the stares and urgent whispers were from one lady to another as they planned to find out the name of Lucinda's hairdresser at the earliest opportunity.

"Lucinda is not to be introduced as my

friend," muttered Ismene to her mother. "Society will think we are making fools of them when it comes out she is only the daughter of a curate. Put it about, Mama, in case the gentlemen ask her to dance and not me."

The countess pressed her daughter's hand reassuringly and moved with determined steps to the row of chaperones to start to inform society about the lowly state of the new beauty. But she had quite forgotten that she had persuaded the patronessses to issue vouchers to the unknown Miss Westerville by creating a false background for Lucinda. As the gossip went about the ballroom, the countess soon found herself faced by one of the angry patronesses, demanding to know why such a cuckoo had been allowed to flutter its feathers in this exclusive nest of the aristocracy. Seeing that her daughter's own vouchers might be at risk, the countess exclaimed that the gossip must have come from some jealous and malicious source. Lucinda was a companion to Ismene, it was true, but of good *ton* and one of the Somerset Westervilles.

She then hurried back to Ismene to warn her that ruining Lucinda socially would mean a termination of Ismene's vouchers. So Ismene was forced to see Lucinda treated as a member of society.

But Lucinda diplomatically turned down many invitations to dance, accepting only when she was sure Ismene had a partner. She was puzzled by Ismene's lack of popularity with the gentlemen. Ismene was beautiful and rich. It was most odd. But Lucinda still considered her own extreme dislike of Ismene as unnatural. The girl was badly spoilt, not a monster. The fact was that Ismene longed for power. She felt secure in her own wealth and attractions and was sure that by saying a great deal of wounding and cutting things to the gentlemen that she was enslaving them the more. So the only partners she had were among the few adventurers and impoverished Irish peers who had slipped in through the iron net of the patronesses' social control.

It was when Ismene, who was dancing with Sir Brian Callaghan, a rakish and penniless Irishman, noticed that Lucinda was being partnered by Lord Peter Trevize, a rich and handsome nobleman, that she felt that matters had gone far enough. So when Lucinda was promenading with Lord Peter at the end of the dance, Ismene walked up to them and said sharply, "Come, companion, you are neglecting your duties."

Lord Peter looked angry and surprised, but Lucinda meekly curtsied and followed Ismene to a line of chairs against the wall. "Now, sit down and stop making a cake of yourself," snapped Ismene. She then sat down angrily next to Lucinda and opened her mouth to give that young lady a severe dressing-down when, fortunately for Lucinda, a diversion happened in the form of a new arrival.

"Here is Rockingham!" cried someone.

The Savage Marquess had just entered the ballroom. Lucinda looked at him curiously. He was handsome in a hard-bitten way, a strong chin and jutting nose, thick black hair, and those odd green eyes under heavy lids. Despite his impeccable English tailoring and the large diamond which blazed from among the snowy folds of his cravat, he looked foreign and out of place among the well-bred English faces. A predator, thought Lucinda, amused despite her distress at Ismene's temper.

He looked haughtily around the ballroom and then stopped to talk to Lady Sally Jersey, one of the patronnesses. She said something which made him laugh, and that laugh transformed his whole face. Not so savage after all, thought Lucinda, feeling breathless. Then the marquess went off in the direction of the card room. Ismene pouted. "He is not going to dance," she said. "Now, Lucinda, here comes that tiresome Mr. Baxter to ask me to dance. You are to stay here and not move!"

Lucinda obediently sat where she was until

the fifth gentleman asked her to dance. She sadly shook her head and then moved to a chair in a far corner behind a group of standing people so that she could hide away in comfort. Shielded at last from the dancers on the floor and from Ismene's accusing stare, Lucinda allowed herself to relax.

She must stop worrying about Ismene. Fear of dismissal was making her timid. Ismene, Lucinda was sure, sensed that timidity and it made her worse. People, mused Lucinda, were sometimes very like wild dogs. If you were afraid of them, they sensed it and moved in for the kill. So she would count her blessings. Papa was being cared for. She herself was in good health and here in that holy of holys, Almack's Assembly Rooms. How furiously jealous the Misses Glossop would be if they could see her now!

A smile crossed Lucinda's face.

The Marquess of Rockingham had quit the card room. He had been about to settle down for a game when he had sternly reminded himself he was on the lookout for a wife. So he had returned to the ballroom to find a country dance in progress. He saw, among the group in front of Lucinda, an acquaintance, Lord Freddy Pomfret, and made his way in that direction.

Lord Freddy's sister, Lady Agatha, looked at the marquess nervously, as if waiting for him to bite. "Back from your travels," said Lord Freddy cheerfully. "London has not seen you this age, but all anyone talks about is that you're on the hunt for a wife. What about Aggie here?"

Lady Agatha, a timid girl with a long nose, murmured, "Oh, Freddy," and looked desperately around the ballroom for escape.

"Everyone's on the hunt here," said the marquess. "I confess I am bored already. I don't like dancing. Why can't I just go up to one of those creatures and say, 'When will we be married?' and cut out all this charade?"

"Got to pretend to be in love," said Lord Freddy easily. He was not in the least afraid of the marquess, being one of the few members of London society who had never been at the receiving end of the marquess's bad temper. He was a tubby, cheerful young man who never strained his brain much with worry or uncertainty. "Only takes a few sighs and letters and then you can call in your lawyers to handle the rest," he pointed out.

"But everyone looks so damned stupid," said the marquess, staring about him with a jaundiced air. The dance ended. To Lady Agatha's relief, a young man asked her to dance. The group about Lord Freddy began to melt away.

And that is when the Marquess of Rockingham first saw Lucinda, sitting against the wall, apparently lost in dreams, a smile on her face. A branch of candles on a shelf above her cast a soft radiance over her burnished hair. Her eyes were wide and dreamy.

"Introduce me," said the marquess, staring at Lucinda.

Lord Freddy turned about. "Can't," he said. "Don't know her. Came in with the Clifton party. Better ask the Countess of Clifton."

"That vain, chattering woman? No." The marquess moved toward Lucinda and stood looking down at her. "Will you dance with me?" he asked.

The dreams left Lucinda's eyes and she looked up at him.

"I am afraid I do not dance," she said.

"Why?"

Ismene's voice came from behind him. "Where is my wretched companion? Ah, Lucinda. There you are. Good evening, Lord Rockingham."

"Who are you?" demanded the marquess.

Ismene blushed and giggled and then said, "I am Ismene, the Earl of Clifton's daughter."

The marquess bowed. "And I am Rockingham. So now we know each other, you may introduce me to this lady."

"Lucinda. My companion."

"Have you no manners, girl?" demanded

the marquess. "Introduce me properly."

"Lucinda, may I present the Marquess of Rockingham. Lord Rockingham, Miss Lucinda Westerville," said Ismene in a thin voice.

Lucinda rose and curtsied.

"Good," said the marquess. "Now leave us alone."

"Yes, run along, Lucinda," said Ismene.

"You. Not her," said the marquess.

Ismene's cheeks flamed. She threw a vicious look at Lucinda and hurried off.

Lucinda glared at the marquess. "My lord, I am a paid companion. Your behavior may have cost me my job."

He looked at her thoughtfully. "I'll give you another job. You may marry me if you like."

Despite her distress, there was something about this abrupt proposal which struck Lucinda as exquisitely ridiculous. She laughed and laughed and finally said in a shaky voice, "No, I thank you, my lord."

"Why not? I am not maimed or crippled. I am titled and rich."

"I do not know you!"

"Do you need to? Oh, let us dance anyway. That's what you ladies expect, is it not?"

"My lord, I have been given instructions not to dance."

"I shall go and tell Clifton to have a word

with that daughter of his. Hey, Clifton!"
roared the marquess.

"No, no," said Lucinda, appalled. "I will
dance with you."

"Good," he said, "but you will find me an
indifferent dancer."

"Then why bother asking me?" said
Lucinda crossly, but one hard hand took hers
while the other pressed firmly at her waist.

"I can feel your bones," remarked the
infuriating marquess. "Why are you so thin?"

"Because my father and I are very poor and
did not often find much to eat," Lucinda said,
deciding to tell the truth and give him a
disgust of her so that he would leave her
alone. "We do not have servants so I
performed the housekeeping duties and
gardening duties myself."

"And now you are companion to Lady
Ismene," said the marquess. "You poor little
thing." He smiled down into her eyes while
his hand tightened at her waist.

Lucinda, who stood at five feet eight inches
in her stocking soles, had never thought anyone would ever call her little. The marquess
was well over six feet. She tried to recall his
bad reputation, but there was something
infinitely comforting about the strength of his
hold on her and something magnetic about
those odd catlike green eyes.

She gave herself up to the enjoyment of the dance and the music.

There were murmurs of surprise and admiration. No one had ever seen the marquess dance so elegantly. The way he looked down at Miss Westerville with a tender, amused look on his face began to make many females think it would be worth trying to see if they could get him to look at them like that.

The dance over, Lucinda retired quickly to her corner. The marquess had enjoyed his dance with her. It had put him in a good mood. He danced and flirted expertly, not knowing his new, charming behavior was rapidly making him the most desired man in London.

Lucinda sat and thought about the feelings she had experienced during that dance with the Marquess of Rockingham. She decided, rather sadly, that the predominant feeling had been one of safety. Most odd.

3

Lucinda sat meekly with her hands folded on her lap, preparing to face Ismene's wrath. Ismene enjoyed bullying—but bullies enjoyed bullying only those who cringed under the lash of their arrogant behavior. Lucinda was determined to be brave.

She was so preoccupied with her thoughts that for some moments she did not realize a gentleman was standing in front of her, looking down at her curiously.

He cleared his throat and Lucinda looked up. She saw a thin, waspish, middle-aged man who looked vaguely familiar.

"Miss Westerville?" ventured this gentleman. "Is it Miss Westerville?"

"Yes, sir. And you . . . ?"

"I am Chamfreys."

Lucinda's face hardened. Now she knew why that face was so familiar. Lord Chamfreys was admittedly no close relative, only her mother's fourth cousin, but he was extremely rich. Lucinda had written him a pathetic little letter begging for help for her father, but had received only a curt note from Lord Chamfreys' secretary saying that his lordship was persuaded that Miss Westerville was overdramatizing the situation and that her father would prove to be merely suffering from a passing ailment.

"What brings you to London?" Lord Chamfreys went on.

"I am working for my living," Lucinda said. "I am companion to Lady Ismene, the Earl of Clifton's daughter."

"A relative of mine . . . working!" exclaimed Lord Chamfreys in horror.

"The Earl of Clifton is taking care of poor Papa and paying his medical expenses in return for my services," said Lucinda primly.

"Indeed! Why was I not informed of this?"

"You were," Lucinda said crossly. "You replied in a pooh-poohing sort of way."

"I," said Lord Chamfreys awfully, "*never* pooh-pooh. What ails your father?"

Lucinda sighed. "He had the French sickness," she said, meaning influenza, "and it left him weak and ill. He needs good food, rest, and medicine, all of which it was not in my power to give him . . . until now."

Ismene came on the scene and interrupted their conversation. Ignoring Lord Chamfreys, whom she judged to be an elderly admirer of her companion, she said harshly, "I told you not to dance, you disobedient girl. If you are going to go on in this wayward manner, then I shall have to tell Papa you are *not at all* suitable."

Lord Chamfreys turned red. "Do you mind introducing yourself, miss?" he said to Ismene. "Miss Westerville is a relative of mine."

Ismene dropped a reluctant curtsy. She was even more furious. A Lucinda with powerful relatives would prove to be a Lucinda harder to bully. She introduced herself. Lord Chamfreys put up his quizzing glass and studied her for some moments while Ismene fidgeted and blushed. "I am Chamfreys," he said at last. He turned to Lucinda. "Good evening to you, Miss Westerville. You shall hear further from us."

The royal "we" thought Lucinda, amused despite her distress. She turned to Ismene. "I know you are cross with me because I danced with Rockingham, but I assure you, had I not, he would have made a scene."

"I am not cross, dear Lucinda," said Ismene with one of her lightning changes of mood. "You must tell me about Rockingham. They say he has had as many mistresses as I have had hot dinners!"

Lucinda felt an irrational stab of disappointment. "He appeared courteous enough," she said. "But you do not want to talk about Rockingham, Lady Ismene. Tell me about your beaux."

Ismene was delighted to oblige. She leaned forward and with many giggled and rolls of the eyes told Lucinda just how many men had been smitten with her charms that evening. "But to return to Rockingham," she said at last. "I do not think he is the ogre he is made out to be. I have a mind to have him for myself."

"If gossip has it right," Lucinda said cautiously, "it appears he simply wants any marriageable female who will put up with him."

"Here he comes!" cried Ismene.

Lucinda saw the marquess bearing purposefully down on them and she knew in her bones that he intended to ask *her* for another dance.

Her large eyes looked straight up into the marquess's with a pleading expression and then flickered sideways in Ismene's direction.

She is begging me to ask that spoilt mistress of hers, thought the marquess crossly. I have no intention of obliging her.

He bowed to both of them, turned on his heel, and strode away. Lucinda let out a little sigh of relief.

"How odd!" Ismene cried. Then she sat pouting. After a few moments she said pettishly, "Is *no one* going to ask me to dance? I declare I do not know what has come over the gentlemen."

"You forget," said Lucinda gently, "we are quite hidden here."

Ismene's face cleared and she jumped to her feet. "Stay where you are," she called back over her shoulder. "There is no need for *you* to dance."

Lucinda drew her chair back farther into the corner. She found herself wishing the Marquess of Rockingham would approach her again, and then immediately wondered why, for such an action on his part would only enrage Ismene.

But, as if in answer to that unspoken wish, the marquess himself appeared before her, holding a glass of lemonade. "Nothing stronger served at Almack's," he said, handing her the glass. Then he brought over a chair and sat down next to her.

"You are placing my job at risk," said Lucinda quietly. "My mistress will not be pleased if she sees you with me."

"A silly, vain girl," said the marquess. He waved an eloquent hand toward the floor. "But then, so are they all."

"You have a harsh opinion of our sex," said Lucinda.

"Yes."

"Then you had better not marry, my lord."

"Oh, I would make a tolerable husband so long as my wife kept out of my way and did not interfere with my pleasures."

"What a bleak prospect." Lucinda looked at him curiously. "Perhaps you might fall in love."

"No, I am too sensible and too honest to dress the desire for heirs up in a pretty name."

"So you think such a tender emotion does not exist, my lord?"

"Undoubtedly it does—for poets, fools, charlatans, and weaklings."

"Then admit to the existence of the higher forms of love—mother love, for instance."

His face became a hard mask. "For such a beautiful creature, you are sadly lacking in brains," he said. He got to his feet. "You are like all the rest of your sex, Miss Westerville. You have a mind filled with trivia and sentimental twaddle."

What an odd world this is, Lucinda thought miserably, watching his retreating back. All at once she felt terribly tired. Would the evening never end!

It was four in the morning before the carriage bore them homeward. Ismene was cross and out of sorts. No one had asked her to dance more than once. Lucinda, seated opposite, was obviously making an effort to keep her eyes open. She should be alert at all times, thought Ismene, glad of a focus for her discontent and anger.

Lucinda was just about to climb into bed when the maid, Kennedy, appeared. "You're to go to Lady Ismene," she said.

"Why?" Lucinda yawned. "Is she ill?"

"Not her. Wants you to read to her."

Lucinda crept wearily through to Ismene's bedroom. The first thing she noticed on entering was the strong aroma of freshly made coffee; the next was the cup in Ismene's hand. In a dazed way Lucinda realized Ismene had noticed her fatigue and had primed herself with strong coffee in order to torment the tired companion with a sleepless night.

If Ismene had struck her, Lucinda could have borne it better. But there was something so cruel and so well-thought-out about such a spiteful action.

There was only one way to cope with Ismene.

"Read to me," Ismene ordered, holding out the first volume of Mary Brunton's *Self-Control.*

"Certainly," said Lucinda brightly, "for I declare I adore novels and could read all night."

Ismene put down her coffee cup and looked sulkily at Lucinda, who started to read.

Although the novel dealt with the improbable adventures of a heroine of quite terrifying righteousness, there were times when any fiction at all was a boon to anyone wanting to escape the harsh realities of the present.

Ismene lay back against the pillows while Lucinda read on with every appearance of great enjoyment.

In fifteen minutes Ismene was fast asleep. Lucinda stopped reading and cast her an amused look.

"I think I know how to deal with you now, my lady," she said in an amused voice as she left the room.

But Lucinda did not yet know the extent of Ismene's talent for humiliation.

The next day, when various gentlemen who had danced with Ismene the night before came to call, as was the custom, Ismene choked off any masculine interest in her pretty companion by dismissing Kennedy and treating Lucinda like a maid, even ordering her to make up the fire.

Lucinda thought of her father and performed all the tasks set her quietly and efficiently.

The Earl of Clifton would certainly have protested against Lucinda's being treated so shabbily, but he had retired to his study and his countess never saw anything wrong in her daughter's behavior at any time.

Then at five o'clock Ismene and Lucinda went off in an open carriage to join the fashionables in the park. There was a brisk wind blowing. Ismene was carrying a dainty parasol. A particularly strong gust seized it out of her hand and blew it across the grass in the direction of the Serpentine. The coachman, hearing Ismene's cry of distress, reined in the horses.

"Go and fetch my parasol, Lucinda," said Ismene. Lucinda cast an eloquent look toward the tall footman on the backstrap, who immediately jumped down.

"Stay, John!" commanded Ismene, stopping the footman in his tracks. "My companion shall fetch it."

Lucinda gave Ismene a startled look, for this was surely persecution beginning to edge on the vulgar. But she climbed down from the carriage and set off in pursuit of Ismene's lilac lace parasol, which was briskly tumbling across the grass.

She picked up her skirts and began to run as hard as she could to try to stop the parasol before it blew into the Serpentine. There came the thud of hooves, a horse flashed in front of her. Its rider bent low and snatched up the parasol, rode a little way away, wheeled about, and cantered back to where Lucinda stood. Lucinda found herself looking up into the mocking eyes of the Marquess of Rockingham. He swung himself down from the saddle, bowed, and held out the lilac parasol. Lucinda took it and thanked him. He called to Chumley, who came riding up. The valet, who accompanied him everywhere, as his lordship's grooms never stayed very long in his employ, dismounted and held the marquess's horse as well as his own.

The marquess fell into step beside Lucinda. "Well, Atalanta," he mocked, "it was indeed a pleasure to watch you in the chase."

"I am grateful to you, my lord," said Lucinda stiffly. "There is no need to accompany me to the carriage."

" 'Where sits our sulky, sullen dame,' " he quoted. "Remark on her courtiers, Miss Westerville, and see how a harsh tongue and an unpleasant disposition will succeed in attracting only man-milliners."

Lucinda saw that Ismene was now holding court to five young exquisites. Their high, mincing voices were borne on the wind. As Lucinda approached with the marquess, Ismene said, "Ah, here is my lazy servant at last. Such a problem finding suitable girls these days."

"La, Lady Ismene," cried one, kissing his fingers, "would I had the honor to be allowed to serve you."

The marquess gently tugged the parasol from Lucinda's hand.

Ismene bestowed on the marquess her most dazzling smile. "Rockingham," she cried, " 'tis most kind of you to help my lazy Lucinda."

A sardonic smile curled the marquess's lips. "Your parasol, I think," he said. He snapped it in two and threw the pieces on the ground.

One of Lucinda's courtiers began to bluster. " Fie, for shame, Rockingham."

"Go on. Call me out," said the marquess nastily.

The five young men began to back away. It was like watching a ballet. With many flourishes of scented handkerchiefs, they continued to edge backward, finally turning as one man and scampering away across the grass.

Tight-lipped, the marquess helped Lucinda into the carriage, bowed to her, and strode away.

Ismene was quite white. "Monstrous man," she said in a shaky voice.

"Shall I fetch the parasol?" asked Lucinda in a quiet voice. "It is pretty and can be repaired."

"No, no," said Ismene, quite terrified. She called to the coachman, "Drive on! Drive on, you great lummox, before he comes back."

Fear kept Ismene silent for the rest of the outing.

But her spirits rallied soon after their return. She instructed the servants to bring a bath up to her bedchamber and then told Lucinda, after the bath was prepared and scented with rosewater, to wash her back.

There was something repellent, Lucinda reflected as she diligently applied a cake of Joppa soap to Ismene's back, about being forced to touch the body of someone you detested. They were to go to the opera that evening. Lucinda felt if she did not have some time to herself, she would break down and scream.

She knew Ismene was trying to humiliate her by her very nakedness. No lady bathed naked, even before a member of her own sex.

"I am so glad we are to go to the opera," said Lucinda gently. "I adore music."

"You do?" Ismene said, her eyes narrowing.

"Oh yes," sighed Lucinda. "It is my greatest pleasure and *Don Giovanni* is my favorite opera."

Ismene shifted irritably in the narrow coffin-shaped bath. "I have some sewing and mending for you, Lucinda," she said. "It is better you remain at home this evening."

"Very good, my lady," Lucinda said in a voice deliberately laden with disappointment, and then turned away so that Ismene should not see the smile of satisfaction on her face.

After Ismene had left for the opera, Kennedy came into Lucinda's bedroom and quietly removed the basket of sewing. "Have a bit of a rest, miss," she said soothingly. "I like sewing and she'll never know it was me who did it."

Lucinda felt a lump growing in her throat. "You are very kind, Kennedy," she said, and added with a sudden burst of candor, "Your life cannot always be easy."

"No, it is not," said the maid. "But it is hard these days for servants to find good positions —unless," she added with a grin, "they want to work for the Marquess of Rockingham. He can never keep anyone."

"Perhaps the living conditions are too cramped," said Lucinda, who knew from remembered gossip she had heard on visits to her rich relatives that aristocrats often kept their money for their country estates and rented only inferior accommodation in town for the Season.

"No, 'tis not that, miss," said Kennedy. "His lordship has a fine town house in Berkeley Square, Number 205, with plenty of spacious rooms, but he is so wild and so dissolute that they all give their notice sooner or later."

Kennedy bobbed a curtsy and left, taking the sewing with her.

Lucinda settled herself in the battered armchair. She reached out to the table beside it, but the novel she had been reading had disappeared. With a cluck of annoyance she went through to Ismene's bedchamber, confident that the girl had borrowed it. But there was no sign of the novel. Lucinda was about to leave when her eye fell on the fireplace. She stiffened. It was full of blackened, burnt paper. Ismene would not . . . could not . . .

She knelt on the hearth. One half-page was all that remained. She pulled out the blackened mess and studied it, and then sat back on her heels, her face white. Ismene had taken her book and had burnt it, the book that had carried a loving inscription from her father on the title page. Such spite was frightening.

"I can't go on," whispered Lucinda. "I can't."

She rose shakily to her feet and went out and downstairs to the library to find something to take her mind away from the horrors of her present situation. She used the back stairs, not wanting to meet the earl, who she knew had stayed behind. The door to the library led off a small landing on the back stairs. A door to the earl's study led from the same landing, the door being opposite the library door. Most rooms in the large mansion had two entrances, one for the servants and one for the masters. She gently put her hand on the knob of the library door. And then she heard the earl's voice coming from behind the study door. He was speaking to a visitor.

"So you see, Cartwright," the earl was saying, "I have nothing against this Miss Westerville myself, but my lady and Ismene are going to make life hell for me until I get rid of her. Ismene came back from her ride in the park and insisted I send Miss Westerville packing by the end of the week."

His voice became louder as he approached the door. Lucinda opened the library door and darted inside, her heart beating hard.

So it was soon to be all over. At the end of the week, she would leave London—but that would mean her father would have to leave the care of Beechings. Hot tears began to run down her cheeks. She must do something. If only someone would help her.

Being her father's daughter, she began to pray for guidance. But when she had finished

her prayers, an idea struck her—a solution—
and she trembled, for such an idea could only
have come from Lucifer himself.

She fled from the library to escape the voice
in her head. She collected Ismene's novel, the
one she had been reading to her, from her
room and forced herself to read the
adventures of surely one of the most tiresome
heroines in English literature.

Had Ismene summoned Lucinda on her
return from the opera, Lucinda might then
have tried to change her mistress's mind
about dismissing her. But Ismene did not.

So when Lucinda awoke early the next
morning, that wretched voice was there, and
louder, urging her on.

"All you have to do," it wheedled, "is to ask
the Marquess of Rockingham to marry you.
No one wants him. No one wants you. A match
made in heaven."

"All *right*," said Lucinda, answering the
inner nagging voice. " 'Fore George! I'll do
it!"

4

LUCINDA'S COURAGE ALMOST deserted her as she walked to Berkeley Square. It was a lovely late-spring morning. The streets were quiet and deserted. An egg-shell-blue sky stretched overhead. Thin lines of smoke were beginning to climb up from the chimneys. Soon London would be covered by its usual ceiling of thin smoke. But for that moment the air seemed to have blown all the way from the country, scented with lilac and early roses.

She had memorized the marquess's address, she realized, the minute Kennedy had mentioned it, almost as if such an outrageous idea had been at the back of her mind from the minute she had first heard of the Savage Marquess's search for a wife.

Lucinda walked twice around the square until the thought of her ailing father stiffened her spine and gave her courage. Rockingham might just laugh at her. But Ismene would not rise until about two in the afternoon and so her job as companion would still be waiting.

She marched to the marquess's town house and stood on the doorstep, looking up at the building.

Her courage deserted her again. Am I merely full of self-pity? wondered Lucinda. I am clothed and fed and my father is taken care of. With a little cunning, I could surely manage Ismene's moods. She changes from moment to moment, and although she has told her father she wants quit of me, she could be made to change her mind. A little judicious flattery, a little fawning, *that* is all that is required. But then the thought of Ismene and everything about her personality filled Lucinda with revulsion.

Choking back a little sob of fright, like the noise a child makes when waking from a bad dream, she seized the knocker and performed a vigorous tattoo on it.

There was a long silence. Then a dust cart went past, the old horse pulling it clop-clopping over the cobbles, a blackbird sang in one of the plane trees in the square behind her, and next door a window shot up and a curious housemaid looked down.

Lucinda hammered on the knocker again.

She was just about to turn away when the door suddenly opened. Chumley stood on the step.

"Yes, miss?" he asked politely, his eyes

quickly taking in the respectability of Lucinda's dress. They roamed behind her as if searching for an accompanying maid, and, finding none, came to rest on Lucinda's face with a tinge of wariness mixed with severity.

"I am come to call on Lord Rockingham," said Lucinda.

"It is very early in the day. I must ask the nature of your business with his lordship."

"A personal matter . . . of . . . of *great* importance."

"Your card, miss?"

Lucinda fumbled in her reticule and took out one of her last, precious calling cards, turned it down at the corner to show she was calling in person, and handed it to Chumley.

His eyes searched her face again. Chumley at last recognized Lucinda as the pretty lady his master had helped in the park.

He hesitated only a moment. "Be so good as to enter, Miss Westerville."

Chumley ushered Lucinda into a gloomy hall and then held open a door leading off it. She found herself in a damp, musty saloon. Chumley bowed and closed the door behind her and then she could hear his footsteps mounting the stairs.

She looked curiously about her. There were some fine chairs, quite modern judging by the fact that all had arms, the new style of lady's and gentlemen's dress allowing for such an addition, whereas the old-fashioned pan-niered gowns and coats with their skirts stiffened with whalebone had not. There was a William Kent bureau, surmounted by an eagle with one outstretched claw on which someone had hung a lady's dusty garter. A backless sofa was placed in front of the fireplace. In front of it stood a sofa table, one of its open drawers revealing several well-thumbed packs of cards. The corners of the floor were still damp, as if the room had been recently scrubbed by a heavy hand and not allowed to air.

Over the fireplace was an oil painting of a stern-faced woman leaning on a pillar, while thunder clouds piled in the sky behind her. She had a nasty little smile on her face.

Lucinda nervously smoothed down her silk pelisse. The fact that the pale blue pelisse was one of Ismene's, changed to fit her thinner figure, gave her a stab of guilt, and once more she wondered whether she was a weakling and a coward, running away to marry a rake.

The door opened and the Marquess of Rockingham walked in. He could hardly be called a pretty sight. His thick black hair was tousled, he was unshaven, and his tall athletic body was wrapped in an Oriental dressing gown gaudily embroidered to the point of decadence. His bare feet were thrust into

Turkish slippers. His green eyes were bloodshot. He had left Almack's and had gone to a gambling hell. A long night's drinking in a smoke-filled room had worked its usual ruin. He had had only a bare two hours' sleep.

He threw Lucinda a jaundiced look, strode over to the sofa and stretched out on it, clasped his hands behind his head, looked up at her, and said, "Well?"

Lucinda looked down at him miserably. This was hardly a Sir Galahad. She doubted if the marquess had one chivalrous thought in his brain.

"I have made a mistake," she said quietly. "I must apologize for troubling you, my lord."

"Don't be silly," he snapped. "You have roused me at this unearthly hour for some reason, you have risked ruining your reputation by calling here, so you had better tell me what it's all about. God, my tongue feels like a carpet." He threw back his head and roared, "Chumley! Chumley! Where are you, you lazy hound?"

The door opened and Chumley came in carrying a tray with a steaming pot of coffee and two cups.

"As usual, Chumley," said the marquess, "you have read my mind. Put it down on the table. Miss Westerville shall serve us."

"Very good, my lord."

The marquess pulled himself upright and patted the sofa beside him. "Sit down, Miss Westerville."

"I . . . I . . . I . . ."

"*Sit down!*"

"There is no need to bark at me," mumbled Lucinda, gingerly sitting on the edge of the sofa. "I am not deaf."

"Pour the coffee and tell me what you are doing here."

Amazed that her hand did not shake, Lucinda poured him a cup of coffee, and then one for herself.

"I came here," she said in a colorless voice, "to ask you to marry me."

"Odso, why? No, no, don't tell me. I think I know. You must escape the clutches of the horrible Ismene. You must provide for your father." He raised a mocking eyebrow at her and quoted:

"Stern daughter of the voice of God!

O Duty! If that name thou love

Who art a light to guide, a rod

To check the erring and reprove."

He studied her face. The wide hazel eyes looked at him miserably.

"Well, I don't see why not," he said. "Pour me another cup of coffee."

Lucinda did as she was bid. "It was bold of me to come here," she said. "Perhaps I should return to my post as companion. Ismene means to send me packing, but I am sure I could flatter her into a good mood."

"Not for long," he said languidly. "You are a deuced sight too pretty."

"Pretty? I?" Lucinda looked at him in surprise.

"Yes," he said, amused. "You. Pretty."

"You do not seem at all surprised by my proposal."

"I shall be when my poor addled brain clears. Have you any conditions? I accept the care of your father."

"Yes," said Lucinda nervously, fiddling with the material of her gown. "I would like six months' grace before we enter into the, er, intimate side of marriage."

"In return for which . . . ?"

"I shall not interfere with your life in any way, but if we can manage together tolerably well, then after six months I shall do my best to give you heirs."

"And if we do not suit?"

"Then the marriage, not consummated, can be easily annulled."

The marquess wondered whether to tell her that he had heard Chamfreys fulminating in the card room at Almack's over the fact that one of his relatives should have to work and had sworn to go to Beechings and remove Mr.

Westerville into his own care. But if he told her that, she would not marry him, and then he should have to go through all the dreary, boring business of courting someone.

"I accept your terms," he said. "Now, hear mine. We will be married today—"

"No!"

"Why not? A little bribery and corruption and I can have a special license in my pocket within the hour. Either you marry me, or you don't. I've accepted your terms, so it's not as if I'm going to drag you to the marriage bed."

Lucinda looked at him, trying to find some hint of compassion or concern behind those mocking green eyes. "Can't we wait?" she asked feebly.

"No. Chumley!" he roared, making Lucinda jump.

When Chumley came in, the marquess said, "Take the required amount of money from my desk and go and get me a special license."

"Yes, my lord."

"I am getting married today to Miss Westerville here. Think you can arrange that?"

"Yes, my lord, provided Miss Westerville is over twenty-one."

"Oh, curse it all. Of course she's not over twenty-one."

"I am . . . just," said Lucinda. "But—"

"There you are, Chumley. Your new

mistress is over twenty-one. Hop to it."

"Very good, my lord."

When he had left, Lucinda said with a weak smile, "I suppose it is rather like going to the dentist. 'If it were done when 'tis done, then 'twere well it were done quickly.' "

"Not an apt quotation. It is marriage you are supposed to be contemplating, not murder."

"I had better return and inform Lady Ismene—"

"No, you may as well stay here. Think of the scenes. Think of the tantrums!"

Lucinda shuddered.

"Well, I had better go and make myself ready. This is your home now. You had better look about. I do not seem to have the knack of keeping servants, so at the moment I am reduced to Chumley and the daily scrubbing women."

He stood up and stretched his arms above his head. His dressing gown fell open to reveal his broad naked chest.

Lucinda quickly looked away. "What have you done?" screamed a voice in her head. But when she looked up again, it was to see him leaving the room.

She sat for a long time, very still, listening to the silence of the house, telling herself that all she had to do was to open the door and run away.

But she thought of her father and she at last forced herself to admit that the marquess had been more than generous in accepting her odd provisos.

A little warm feeling of gratitude toward this odd rake began to spread through her body. She decided to explore, and went down to the kitchens first.

She looked in dismay at the greasy black hole that was the main kitchen. There was an antiquated open range for cooking, a rough table covered in old scraps of food, greasy walls and dirty china and filthy pots. Obviously it had not been used for cooking anything lately. The hearth was cold. Chumley must have made the coffee on a spirit stove abovestairs. There was a tolerably clean baize apron hanging behind the door. Lucinda took off her pelisse and bonnet, tied on the apron, and proceeded to light the fire. A little scrubbing and cleaning would take her mind off her fast-approaching nuptials.

The marquess had shaved himself and dressed by the time Chumley returned and silently handed him a special license and a gold ring. "Where am I to be married?" asked the marquess.

"St. Edmund's in Dove Lane, Holborn, my lord."

"I suppose it will have to do. Hardly the most salubrious neighborhood. You had better be brideman, Chumley. Can you raise some female to act as maid of honor to Miss Westerville?"

"I have already arranged for a Mrs. Grant, a sidesman's wife, to perform that service."

"You may raise your wages, Chumley."

"Your lordship is most kind. There is one problem, however. . . "

"That being . . . ?"

"Miss Westerville is no longer in the saloon."

"If that silly unmentionable epithet has fled the coop, I shall track her down and wring her neck."

"May I say, my lord, Miss Westerville did not strike me as the sort of lady to do anything so impolite. Had she changed her mind, then I am sure she would have informed your lordship first."

The marquess stood frowning. Then he said, "Follow me."

He clattered down the stairs with Chumley after him. To Chumley's surprise, his master continued on down the back stairs to the kitchens.

"I thought so," said the marquess with satisfaction.

Chumley peered over his master's shoulder.

The fire was blazing in the kitchen range.

The table was scrubbed, and shining dishes gleamed in serried ranks on the dresser. From the scullery came the sound of splashing water.

The marquess, followed by Chumley, walked through to the scullery. Lucinda was diligently scrubbing pots.

"I want a wife, not a slave," said the marquess.

Lucinda straightened up and brushed a damp tendril of hair from her forehead. "I will not be able to engage any kitchen staff if the place is left in the disgusting mess in which I found it."

"May I say, my lord," put in Chumley, "that the mistress has the right of it. The last house-keeper I tried to engage took one look at the state of the place and had the vapors."

"Then why didn't you clean up the place yourself, man?"

"Because in a servantless house, I have a damn sight too much to do as it is, my lord," snapped Chumley.

Lucinda waited, trembling, for the marquess's wrath to break over poor Chumley, although surely such insolence from a mere servant deserved any master's wrath.

The marquess contented himself with casting a malevolent look at his valet. "Are you going to stand there delivering yourself of jaw-me-deads all day? Or are you going to see me married?"

"We shall leave as soon as the mistress is ready."

"She's not the mistress yet and won't be if someone doesn't hurry up!"

"Come with me, Miss Westerville," said Chumley.

Lucinda followed the valet out and up the stairs to the dusty bedchamber. A toilet table had been hurriedly cleaned and supplied with cans of water and fresh towels.

"Thank you, Chumley. Is it so hard to get servants?"

"Yes, miss, but a lady in the house will make life different."

He bowed and withdrew.

With the cleaning of the kitchen, Lucinda felt she had burnt her boats. The work had kept her frightened thoughts at bay. A calm descended on her as she washed her face, brushed her hair, and straightened her dress.

When she entered the saloon to join the marquess, she noticed he looked tolerably healthy and his eyes were clear. He appeared relaxed and amused.

She tied on her bonnet and allowed Chumley to help her into her pelisse, both of which she had left in the kitchen.

The marquess held out his arm, his green eyes glinting down at her.

She timidly took his arm. "There you are!" he said bracingly. "We look quite like an old married couple already."

From then on the day took on an even more unreal appearance for Lucinda. She felt as if she were acting in a play. The church was dark and smelly and her maid of honor, a squat, mannish woman, reeked of gin. Lucinda had attended many weddings with her father and knew the service by heart, but the marquess needed to be prompted. He became cross and fidgety and began to exude a restless air of boredom.

When they were finally declared man and wife, he planted a brief and careless kiss on Lucinda's cold mouth and led her hurriedly from the church.

"Thank God, that's over. If I'd known what an infernal bore it was going to be, I doubt if I'd have faced up to it."

"Where to, my lord?" asked Chumley as they climbed into the carriage. Chumley was acting as coachman.

"We'd better go to Clifton's," said the marquess.

"No," protested Lucinda.

"Why not? You need your bits and pieces,

and Ismene can hardly eat you with me around."

Ismene was in a sulky temper, which was growing worse by the minute. She had been informed sometime earlier by Kennedy that Lucinda had gone out and had not returned. She had descended to her father's study to tell him of Lucinda's thoughtless and selfish behavior, only to find her father closeted with Lord Chamfreys.

"If you see Miss Westerville," said the Earl of Clifton to his pouting daughter, "tell her that Chamfreys is taking Mr. Westerville into his care and will take Miss Westerville with him when he goes to the country."

This, of course, added to Ismene's fury. The Cliftons had no hold over Lucinda now.

She was pacing up and down the drawing room, thinking out ways to make Lucinda's life utterly miserable before she left, when a footman popped his head around the door and asked in a worried voice whether the Earl of Clifton was available.

"I don't know where he is, James," said Ismene crossly. "Try the library or the study. Is someone called to see him?"

"The Marquess of Rockingham, miss, and—"

"Send the marquess in here, immediately," cried Ismene.

The footman bowed and withdrew. The countess, Ismene's mother, then fluttered in.

"Mama!" cried Ismene. "Do but listen! Rockingham has called and is asking for Papa. He means to propose."

"Then he must be sent packing," said the countess.

"No, he must not," said Ismene, stamping her foot. "He is rich and handsome and I want him."

Behind her, the footman once more opened the door.

In a loud voice he cried, "His most noble lordship, the Marquess of Rockingham, and Lady Lucinda, Marchioness of Rockingham."

And that was when Ismene began to scream.

5

A QUARTER OF AN hour later, while the sounds of Ismene's hysterics still resounded through the house, Lucinda sat in a corner of the Earl of Clifton's study and heard with a sort of numbness that Lord Chamfreys had already made arrangements to care for her father.

The earl had burst in upon the scene in the drawing room, had slapped his daughter for the first time, and had had his hair pulled by his enraged countess. Extricating himself from the grip of his angry wife, the earl had ordered the marquess and Lucinda to follow him to his study. There he told the marquess that, as he was in effect Lucinda's employer, he should be told the reason for this rushed wedding. The earl's eyes cast a cynical look at Lucinda's waistline, quite forgetting that if Lucinda had fallen from grace, she would hardly be showing signs of a pregnancy after a few days in London.

In a bored, insulting voice, the marquess said that he and Lucinda had come to the arrangement of marriage because he wanted a wife and couldn't be bothered with the fatigue of looking for one, and that Lucinda found her life as companion to the Lady Ismene quite horrible.

The Earl of Clifton gave a little sigh. He felt he should cry out against this insult to his daughter, but, under the gaze of the marquess's world-weary eyes, found he could not. Then he told Lucinda of his recent visit from Lord Chamfreys.

Lucinda sat twisting the gold wedding ring on her finger. She need never have gone through with this charade of a marriage. Now she was trapped. But through her misery like a ray of sunlight came the sudden thought that Lord Chamfreys in his way was as unreliable a prop as the Cliftons. Should her father fail to rally quickly, then Lord Chamfreys might quickly become bored with the responsibility of looking after him.

"Well, that appears to be that," said the marquess restlessly. "Would you be so good, Clifton, as to have my wife's belongings sent to our address?"

He rose to his feet. Wife, thought Lucinda. How . . . final.

They traveled in silence to Berkeley Square. "Make yourself at home," said the marquess abruptly. "I'm going out. Be back sometime. Come along, Chumley."

The valet hesitated. He thought it was a bit hard on the new marchioness to be abandoned in a servantless house, but he knew the marquess would quickly become savagely bad-tempered if forced to stay at home.

Left to herself, Lucinda wandered through the empty rooms, wondering what to do, hoping desperately that this new, erratic husband of hers might not decide to get drunk and forget his promise of leaving her free of marital duties for six months.

She took off her bonnet and pelisse and then went down to the kitchen to resume cleaning. Hard work would keep her mind off her troubles.

She scrubbed and washed and polished until every plate and pot and pan was shining. There did not seem to be any food at all in the house. She was about to go upstairs to continue her labors when she heard a tremendous knocking at the street door.

Half-afraid it might be Ismene calling to continue berating her, Lucinda went reluctantly to answer it. A liveried footman stood on the step. "I have a mesage for the Marchioness of Rockingham," he said loftily.

"I am she," said Lucinda, blushing slightly as the footman's haughty stare changed to one of amazement as he surveyed my lady in all the glory of tousled hair and baize apron.

He bowed and handed her a letter. "Are you to wait for a reply?" Lucinda asked.

"No, my lady," the footman said. His hand was outstretched. But Lucinda did not have any money to tip him. She smiled instead and shut the door in his face. She carried the letter into the saloon and sat down and began to read it. At first she could not believe her eyes, so she read it again.

In a bold scrawl, her husband had written: "Gone to Paris for a time. There is money in the desk in my room but everyone will give you credit. Rockingham."

Lucinda burst into angry tears. It was too much! She stared through the blur of her tears at the grim room, and became aware of the lonely, oppressive silence of the house.

There was only one thing to do—throw herself on Lord Chamfrey's mercy.

She was about to go upstairs to look for the money in the desk so that she would be able to pay for a seat on the stagecoach, when there came another volley of knocking at the door.

Hoping against hope that it might prove to be the marquess, she ran to answer it. Kennedy stood on the step, her eyes red with weeping.

"Why, Kennedy!" exclaimed Lucinda, falling back a step so as to allow the maid to enter. "What's amiss?"

"My lady pulled my hair and scratched my face," said Kennedy, turning her left cheek to show Lucinda the marks of the attack. "She said it was all my fault—that if I had not prettified you so much, you would never have caught the eye of Rockingham. I could not bear it any longer. I am come to ask you, my lady, if you be in need of servants."

"Oh, I am. I am," said Lucinda gratefully. "Come in, Kennedy." She opened the door of the saloon and ushered the maid in. "I cannot even offer you tea. I am sure Chumley has some hidden somewhere, but I cannot find it. I was about to run away to the country, but now, if you will help me, perhaps I might be able to manage. I have no servants *whatsoever.*"

"But where is my lord, your husband?"

"He has upped and gone off to Paris and taken his only servant with him, Kennedy, so I am quite alone and do not know where to begin. We need meat and groceries and a full staff of servants."

"So you will engage me, my lady?"

"Yes, Kennedy. You will be lady's maid, after we get other servants."

"I shall return to Lord Clifton's," said Kennedy, "and I'll collect my things. Then I shall call on the butcher and grocer. Then I shall call at Mrs. Pembery's residence in

Mount Street. I have heard that her butler, a good man, is unhappy in her employ. I know Lord Rockingham found it nigh impossible to engage servants, but with his lordship away, and with you being the marchioness, it should not be difficult. If I can get this butler—Humphrey, his name is—if I can get him, then he in turn can engage suitable people."

"But he will be unable to leave just like that! And what about you, Kennedy? Lady Ismene will not allow you to walk out just like that."

"I know how to make her throw me out," said Kennedy grimly. "I am going back to tell her exactly what I think of her. Humphrey will no doubt do the same with Mrs. Pembery."

"You seem like a tower of strength, Kennedy. I declare I shall stay and fight after all."

It was a weary Lucinda who finally crawled into bed in the small hours after having sent a letter to her father telling him of her marriage. She told him she was madly in love with the marquess. She did not want him to think she had married Rockingham for any other reason.

Lucinda had selected a bedchamber for her use on the floor above her husband's quarters. Kennedy had arrived back with the glad news that Humphrey and several of Mrs. Pembery's other disaffected servants would be arriving in the morning to take up their duties.

Before she fell into an exhausted sleep, Lucinda's one comforting thought was that London society would probably not learn about her marriage for some time, since her reprehensible husband had gone off without making any announcement.

In this, Lucinda was wrong.

Before leaving for Paris, the marquess had sent Chumley off with the announcement to be placed in the *Morning Post*. He kept a change of clothes in his club and he had set out for Paris with only those, having experienced a reluctance to return to Berkeley Square. The novelty of his wedding had quickly worn off and he wondered hazily whether he were mad.

So several society breakfasts were ruined by the announcement of his marriage.

The marquess's mistress, Mrs. Maria Deauville, could not believe her eyes. Her plump little hands holding the newspaper began to shake. But she convinced herself it was all a hum. One of Rockingham's little jokes. No one who was anyone had heard of a

Miss Westerville. Still, she could not be easy until she had seen him.

The Honorable Zeus Carter felt all hope go out of his life when he saw the *Morning Post* with that terrible announcement. He thought miserably of his bills. He knew he was able to command vast credit due to his expectations. He was not the only person who expected the marquess to meet an early death. His only hope was that the marquess had been abysmally drunk when he had proposed and had fixed his interest on a female beyond the years of childbearing. Misery loves company and Mr. Carter craved the company of someone who was likely to feel as miserable as he did himself. He crawled from bed, determined to call on Maria Deauville at the first opportunity.

The marquess's parents, the Duke and Duchess of Barnshire, had just taken up residence in their own town house in Grosvenor Square. They had not bothered themselves much about their eldest son since the day he was born, except to see that he was firmly disciplined on all occasions. But the fact that their son had upped and married a nobody made the duchess quite apoplectic with rage. She called for her maid and began a lengthy toilette, as if putting on armor before going into battle.

* * *

Lucinda was flushed and busy and beginning to enjoy herself. The new butler was quiet and competent and had arrived with two housemaids, and wonder upon wonders, a cook. Footmen and more maids and kitchen staff were hired from an agency, the agency confident that things must have taken a turn for the better now that the wicked and unruly marquess was married.

She had just ordered the footmen to take down the picture of the lady with the sinister smile which hung over the fireplace in the saloon and put it in the attic when she received her first caller. It was the Duchess of Barnshire. Humphrey, knowing his mistress was wearing an old gown and apron, tried to keep the duchess in the hall while he warned Lucinda of her arrival, but the angry duchess pushed past him and strode into the saloon.

"Where is my son?" she shouted. "What have you done with my son? And where, may I ask, is this new wife of his?"

Taking off her apron and handing it to Kennedy, Lucinda said quietly, "I was married to your son yesterday, your grace."

"*You*," said the duchess in accents of loathing. She looked Lucinda up and down, from her worn shoes to her hair, which was tied up with a ribbon.

"Furthermore," said Lucinda, "Rockingham has gone to Paris."

"Paris!"

"Yes, Paris," Lucinda said patiently.

The duchess moved forward and sat down on the sofa, her back ramrod straight. She was a tall woman with a grim face and a mouth that seemed to be perpetually curved in a nasty smile. Seeing that smile, Lucinda involuntarily glanced at the empty area over the fireplace where the portrait had hung.

"And where is my portrait?" asked the duchess.

"In the attics, your grace."

"Why, pray?"

"I did not like it," said Lucinda, too rattled to do other than tell the stark truth.

"You . . . did . . . not . . . like . . . it?" said the duchess awfully.

"Well, er, no, as a matter of fact."

The duchess took a deep breath. "There is something havey-cavey about this marriage and I am going to get to the bottom of it. Are you with child?"

"Don't be impertinent," Lucinda said crossly.

"If you are not with child, then why did he marry you?"

"Because I asked him to," said Lucinda. "Your grace, your son went off directly after our wedding, leaving me along in a house without either food or servants. I have much to do. I suggest you take your leave and I shall inform my husband on his return of your call. He will no doubt be pleased to explain his reasons for marrying me."

The duchess stood up, quivering with rage. "You are a nobody, my pert miss. A nobody. And if you had any hopes of cutting a dash with the *ton*, you had best forget it. No one will receive you without my approval. No one."

"Good," said Lucinda. "For Rockingham's idea of a pigsty for a home is not mine, and he has left me much work to do. Humphrey, the door. Her grace is just leaving."

When the door closed behind the duchess, Lucinda said ruefully to Kennedy, "I dealt with that visit very badly. How did she learn so quickly? Oh, Rockingham must have called on her before he left for Paris."

"Perhaps it was because an announcement of your marriage appeared in the newspapers this morning," put in Humphrey.

Lucinda's lips tightened. How thoughtless of Rockingham to do such a thing and then leave town. Surely he would know he was leaving her to face angry family and curious callers alone.

"I had better change," she said. "I wonder who will be next?"

* * *

Mrs. Deauville was just descending the stairs of her elegant mansion in Montague Street when Mrs. Zeus Carter arrived, flushed and breathless.

Maria's heart sank when she saw him. A distressed Mr. Carter surely meant the announcement was not a joke.

"It is terrible! Terrible!" cried Mr. Carter.

"Rockingham's marriage?" said Maria. "A jest, surely."

Mr. Carter took out a handkerchief the size of a lace bedspread and mopped his brow. "I fear it is the truth," he said. "Rockingham told me he intended to wed."

An ugly flush spread over Maria's white neck. "Come into the drawing room," she said. "I would hear more of this."

Mr. Carter tittuped in after her on the high heels of his boots. He waited until she was seated and then leaned romantically against the mantel, one finger pointing to his brow.

Despite his distress, he did hope Mrs. Deauville admired his latest Attitude, which was that of Noble Poet in the Grip of the Muse. But Maria was too distressed. He gave up his pose and looked at her. She was an enchanting creature, small and dainty, with a cascade of blond curls bound with a blue filet, large childlike blue eyes, and a perfect figure. She must be nearly thirty, marveled Mr.

Carter, and yet she looked barely twenty-one. He had met her before on several occasions.

"He said nothing to me about wanting to get married," said Maria. "Nothing."

"Perhaps he was in his cups and sent off the advertisement to tease everyone," said Mr. Carter. "That is what he would do, you know."

Maria's face cleared. "There is still hope," she said. "I was on my way to call. He will be furious with me, for I have never called at his home before. But he will understand."

"If he is married, it ruins all my hopes of being his heir," said Mr. Carter. He thought of the money the marquess had given him. He should have used some of it to settle his more pressing debts, but instead, he had bought himself a new carriage lined with blue silk and a team of matching white horses to pull it. There was plenty left over, even after this extravagance, but it went against the grain to pay a lot of vulgar duns. Mr. Carter blanched as he realized they would now be even more pressing. And no one would give him any credit if it were believed he had no longer any hopes of inheriting any money.

"Perhaps it would be as well if I did not call," said Maria thoughtfully. "It will not look at all odd if you go to pay your respects, and then you can return here and tell me whether it is true or not."

"What shall we do if it *is* true?" asked Mr. Carter.

There was an edge to Maria's silvery tones as she said, "Marriages can be broken, you know. Go, and return as soon as possible."

Mr. Carter went on his way. He had quite convinced himself that it was one of Rockingham's jokes by the time he reached Berkeley Square.

The first sign of impending disaster was when a polite and correct butler answered the door. "Where's Chumley?" asked Mr. Carter, handing his card.

Humphrey bowed. "If by Chumley you mean his lordship's valet, then he is no doubt with his lordship in Paris."

"Paris?" echoed Mr. Carter weakly.

Taking a deep breath, he summoned up all his courage. "Her ladyship at home?" he asked as casually as he could, although he noticed to his irritation that his voice trembled.

"I shall ascertain if her ladyship is at home."

He walked away up the stairs, leaving Mr. Carter standing in the hall.

Mr. Carter looked about him gloomily. The hall, he noticed, was clean and shining. Worse than that, there was a beautiful arrangement of spring flowers on a side table.

He could hear a murmur of voices coming from abovestairs. After a few moments, Humphrey descended.

"I regret her ladyship is not available, sir."

I must see her, thought Mr. Carter wildly. I must see who has stolen my inheritance.

"Perhaps," he said with a little laugh, "her ladyship is not aware that I am Lord Rockingham's cousin and, perhaps, his closest friend and adviser."

"I shall convey that piece of intelligence to her ladyship," said Humphrey.

Mr. Carter began to pace up and down, nervously chewing at the tip of one deerskin-gloved finger. This time Humphrey took longer.

At last he came back. "Follow me, sir," he said. He led the way up the stairs to the second floor and opened the door of the drawing room. Mr. Carter remembered that the drawing room had barely been used by the marquess. The ground-floor saloon was the one in which the marquess received any callers.

The drawing room was full of vases of flowers. It smelled fresh and sweet and had lost its old aroma of cheroots, coal smoke, and stale brandy.

The door opened and Lucinda entered. Mr. Carter's first emotion was one of surprise. How could Rockingham have married such an undistinguished-looking creature with such a lovely as Maria Deauville around?

In order to give herself dignity, Lucinda had tucked her hair up under a cap. She was wearing a severe gown of dark brown tabby. She was very thin, Mr. Carter noticed, and her mouth was too large. Fashion decreed that all ladies must have the tiniest of mouths, and Mr. Carter was fashion's slave.

"Mr. Carter?" asked Lucinda, holding his calling card between her fingers.

Mr. Carter made his best bow, flourishing his handkerchief and dragging his right leg along the floor with a tremendous scrape. "I am Mr. Carter, ma'am, Rockingham's cousin."

"I am delighted to meet you," lied Lucinda, who had taken a dislike to this effeminate fribble on sight.

"You see before you," said Mr. Carter, striking his thin chest, "Rockingham's cousin and boon companion."

What a lot of counts I am learning against my husband, thought Lucinda. Selfish, drunken, and, if Mr. Carter is indeed his boon companion, weakling and fool.

Lucinda decided to bring the visit to a

98

speedy end. "I regret I cannot offer you any refreshment, Mr. Carter," she said. "I am much engaged in housecleaning."

Mr. Carter ignored this. "I was surprised to hear of your marriage," he said, "and hurt to the quick. I would have thought Rockingham would have seen fit to invite me."

"Rest assured, Mr. Carter, he did not invite anyone. If you desire any explanation of our marriage, although I am sure a gentleman such as yourself would not even think to be so impertinent, then I suggest you wait until Rockingham's return from Paris."

Mr. Carter threw her a baffled look. She was undoubtedly a lady. But too haughty and high in the instep. He longed to take her down a peg. Perhaps, he thought suddenly, she might be blissfully ignorant of the rakish character of her husband. "One has only to look at you, ma'am," he said with another elaborate bow, "to see that your looks, your figure, you face, are explanations in themselves. But I am here to introduce myself to you as your new friend. Call on me for assistance at any time, I beg you. A word of warning. Do not receive Mrs. Maria Deauville should she call. She is dying with rage, of course."

"Who is Mrs. Deauville?" Lucinda had forgotten Ismene's gossip.

"Why, Rockingham's mis . . . La, my naughty tongue. Servant, ma'am, servant. I shall call on you again soon."

He flourished his way out.

Spiteful, horrible man, thought Lucinda. Mr. Carter had been about to say this Mrs. Deauville was her husband's mistress.

"Well, I don't care," Lucinda said aloud. "He can have scores of mistresses so long as he takes care of Papa. What a good thing I am not in love with him!"

6

THE MARQUESS, WHO, like many British people, had journeyed across the Channel for the first time in eleven years, nearly turned back at Dieppe.

With Napoleon incarcerated on Elba, France was once more wide open to English visitors. But whereas England had forged ahead, France seemed depressingly old-fashioned. Unlike Brighton with its graceful terraces facing the ocean, its libraries and shops, Dieppe was still a medieval town with its back to the sea and sewers flowing down its muddy streets. The marquess was assailed by packs of beggars, proudly displaying their open sores, and poor sticklike children who followed his carriage, crying out curses against Napoleon in the hope that the English milord would throw them money.

The marquess had tucked his marriage to Lucinda firmly in the back of his mind, but occasionally her face rose before his eyes, and he cursed himself for his stupid folly in allying himself with an innocent country girl whom he hardly knew. So he forged on in the direction of Paris through a countryside where time appeared to have stood still for a century. He stayed at grand posting houses with gilt furniture and greasy floors, unswept hearths, and piles of horse dung at the doors. The countryside appeared to have been depopulated by the wars and there were twelve women working by the roadside to every man.

The entrance into Paris was even more depressing. At the northern gate there was a rough wooden palisade guarded by red-capped soldiers with dangling earrings. Then his carriage moved through a labyrinth of high, crazy, crumbling medieval houses with pointed roofs and fantastic gables, shutting out the sky.

Now that war and plunder had ceased, the residents of this bloody and ferocious capital city had thrown themselves into hectic, shameless gaiety, with all the energy they had used in battle and revolution.

The wild mood of Paris suited the marquess's mood. There were gastronomic paradises such as Very's, Hardi's, and the Quadron Bleau to be visited. Gambling was a universal relaxation with both sexes crowded into airless rooms where no sound was heard but the rattling of dice and money. The English visitors, who had hitherto considered London the center of gambling, were shocked by the intensity of the play and the huge sums which were wagered night after night. To them this gambling frenzy appeared even more shocking than the pornographic prints on the walls of their hotel rooms.

The marquess plunged into this devil-take-tomorrow world and forgot he was a married man. But his pleasures were gambling, dancing, and eating, not women. He was just beginning to become jaded after two weeks' dissipation when Maria Deauville tracked him down. It had been easy for Zeus Carter and Maria to work out that the marquess's marriage had not been consummated. They had been clever enough not to bribe Lucinda's servants, for bribed servants, they both knew, often took the money and then told their mistresses and masters of the bribe, therefore gaining more money for their honesty. Instead, Maria's own maid, Benson, had befriended Kennedy. Kennedy, who had had no friends during her time with Lady Ismene, was glad of company on her afternoon off. Benson was normally never allowed any time off at all, but had been granted the same liberty as Kennedy so that she might extract useful pieces of gossip.

The sight of the charming Maria did not please the marquess.

She came sweeping, unannounced, into his bedchamber one morning.

The marquess struggled up against the pillows with a smile on his face, a smile which was quickly replaced with a scowl. For just at that moment, Lucinda's face came between his own and Maria's.

The fact that he had behaved irresponsibly and disgracefully struck him like a blow. In that moment, he decided he must return to London.

"My sweet," he said to Maria, "what brings you here?"

"The same as yourself," she said with a charming laugh. "To enjoy myself."

Maria had decided to make no mention of his marriage until she had him safely in her arms again.

The marquess thought quickly. He wanted to avoid a scene, and he was sure Maria planned to make one sooner or later.

"Do but leave me to wash and dress," he said. "Come back this afternoon."

"At what time?" asked Maria.

"Oh, I don't know. Say three o'clock?"

Maria's eyes narrowed a fraction. The marquess's catlike eyes regarded her blandly. "You are arrived monstrous early," he said gently.

"Oh, very well. I shall return at three." She walked over to the bed and bent to kiss him, but the marquess chose exactly that moment to yell, "Chumley!" and the valet entered the room very promptly, almost as if he had been waiting outside the door.

"I need to get dressed," said the marquess. "But first, show Mrs. Deauville downstairs."

Chumley bowed and held open the door. Maria threw the marquess a baffled look, but went out, followed by Chumley.

She came after me, thought the marquess. She knows of my marriage and yet said nothing. That means trouble. Her very clothes spelled trouble. She was dressed like a vicar's wife and not like a courtesan. So, let me think. That means she wishes to show me that she is of marriageable stamp. But why? I *am* married. Ah, but she has no doubt learned of my departure immediately after the wedding and has guessed the marriage to be unconsummated, and such a marriage could be easily made null and void. I wonder if she called on Lucinda.

That last thought gave him a painful stab of guilt. Then he began to think of all the others who would most definitely have called on Lucinda—his mother for one.

When Chumley came back into the room, the marquess asked him, "Am I a monster of irresponsibility, Chumley?"

Chumley opened a drawer containing clean cravats. "Yes, my lord."

"Then why do you stay with me?"

"Your lordship's irresponsibility stops short of myself. I am well paid."

"Then earn your keep by making sure we are ready for the road to London by noon."

The staff of the hotel had reason to curse the thoughtless marquess by three that afternoon when Mrs. Deauville threw one of the worst scenes they claimed they had witnessed since the Terror—although trying to pull the manager's hair out by the roots was hardly the same as a beheading.

It was unfortunate, reflected Chumley, that his master had met up with such a bunch of rogues on the road home. At Dieppe was a party of bucks and bloods also bound for London. The ship that was to take them across the Channel was delayed for two days, and in those two days the marquess drank deep with his new friends and gambled heavily. The drinking and gambling then continued on board ship and then on the long dusty road to London. One of the party suggested they enliven their arrival with a party graced by a few ladies of cracked reputation. This was hailed with enthusiasm, and the marquess, his green eyes glittering with a hectic light, suggested his town house in Berkeley Square for the event. All remorse over his cavalier treatment of Lucinda had gone.

It was ten in the evening when Lucinda heard the first warning sounds of their impending arrival. She had heard similar sounds of drunken revelry most nights, but for some reason she sensed this row was about to descend on her. She went to the window of the drawing room and looked down.

A line of dusty carriages was drawing to a halt outside. The first down was her husband. He staggered slightly as he reached the pavement. Then came a crowd of highly painted, scantily dressed ladies and boozy bucks.

Lucinda looked wildly around what she had come to consider as her home. New furniture gleamed in the soft light of oil lamps. Silver, china, and glass sparkled. Flowers gave splashes of color to the rooms and scented the air.

I married a rake, she thought sadly. And I had near forgot.

She looked down at her new gown of pale blue muslin. Her hair had grown longer in the weeks the marquess had been away and she had dressed it in one of the latest Grecian styles. She had put on some much-needed weight and the low line of her gown revealed the upper quarter of two perfectly shaped white breasts.

She marched down the steps, waved Humphrey, the butler, to one side, and opened the door. The party, headed by the marquess, who had been about to enter, stopped and stared at her.

"Good evening, my lord," said Lucinda calmly. "Welcome home."

"You are beautiful!" said the marquess, blurting out the first thing that came into his head.

"Thank you, my lord." Lucinda looked haughtily at the motley crowd clustered behind her husband. "Good night," she said firmly. She took the marquess's arm so that she could draw him inside and shut the door on his company.

A wicked gleam darted into the marquess's eyes. "Quite the mistress of the household, my love." He sneered. "Well, carry out your duties. These are my friends. "He opened the door again. "Come along, everybody."

There was a noisy cheer and with a charge they all shoved past Lucinda, pushing her to one side.

One man immediately suggested they play a game called Chase the Doxy. The prostitutes giggled and took flight with the men hallooing after them.

The marquess went into the downstairs saloon and began to pull off his boots. "Get us champagne, Chumley," he roared. Then he looked around him and blinked. Lucinda stood in the doorway watching him. The marquess looked at the new delicate furniture, at the ornaments and flowers, the shining polish on the floorboards, and smelled the delicate scent of flowers and rosewater.

From upstairs came screams followed by the sound of breaking glass. Lucinda did not move. She stood where she was, watching her husband.

Chumley had not left to get the champagne. He stood surveying his master and mistress.

The marquess suddenly sprang to his feet. "Get 'em out, Chumley. Fast."

The valet's face creased in a wide grin. "Certainly, my lord."

The marquess sat down again and leaned back in the new comfortable armchair and closed his eyes. "Come in, Lucinda, and close the door behind you," he said quietly.

Lucinda came in and sat in a chair opposite him. He remained there with his eyes closed as the sound of screams and curses came down from upstairs to the hall, then into the street, and then there came the sounds of carriages being driven away.

Peace fell on the house. The marquess opened his eyes and sighed.

"My apologies, my love," he said in a slightly slurred voice. "You see, I did not know I was coming back to a home."

And with that, he fell fast asleep.

Chumley came in at last with the champagne. "We do not need that now," said Lucinda. "I am going to bed. I suggest you get your master to his."

When she got to her own bedchamber, Lucinda realized she was trembling with shock. She sat down on the bed and picked up the letter she had received from her father. It had arrived two weeks ago, but Lucinda had read it over and over again. Lord Chamfreys had obviously told Mr. Westerville nothing of the marquess's reputation, only of his fortune. Mr. Westerville had written that he had been at first distressed because Lucinda had not waited for his recovery before becoming wed to the Marquess of Rockingham. But on calmer reflection, Mr. Westerville said, he had realized that the marriage was an answer to his prayers. That Lucinda should gain title and fortune and love as well was a true blessing from God.

He will know sooner or later I have married

a rake, thought Lucinda sadly. But let me pray that by that time he will be strong enough to bear the news.

After she had said her prayers, she undressed and prepared herself for bed. She was just about to climb into bed when the door crashed open and her husband strode into the room. "What are you doing here?" Lucinda screamed.

"I am coming to bed with you," he said, unwinding his cravat.

"You promised me you would wait for six months."

"I don't want to wait."

"You, sir, are no gentleman."

"You should have known that when you married me. Come here."

"No."

The marquess took a flying leap and landed on the bed, driving nearly all the breath out of her body. Then he pulled her roughly into his arms and forced her chin up.

"You enchant me," he said huskily.

"Faugh!" Lucinda said, wrinkling her nose. "What a disgusting smell."

The gleam of drunken lust died in the marquess's eyes, to be replaced with a comical one of pure amazement. "What smell?" he asked.

"You," Lucinda said. "You smell of stale

brandy, new champagne, sweat, cigars, and—pooh!—when did you last take a bath?"

Despite his reputation, the marquess had never experienced any trouble from any woman once he had taken her in his arms. Lucinda's words had the effect on him of a pail of cold water being thrown over his head.

"I am sorry my body offends you," he said stiffly.

"Offends *me*," said Lucinda. "My lord, it would offend the whole of a city. You are quite rank."

The marquess swung his legs off the bed, straightened up, and glared at her. "You little whining virgin," he said. "How dare you insult me."

"I speak no more than the truth," Lucinda said breathlessly.

He marched to the door, went out, and slammed it viciously behind him.

After a few moments, Lucinda heard him roaring for Chumley to have a bath carried up.

She lay there for a long time shaking and trembling, quite sure he would come back after he had washed. But the night wore on, and the watch was calling two in the morning before Lucinda fell into an exhausted sleep.

In the morning, Lucinda awoke and rang for

Kennedy. When the maid appeared, she said, "Kennedy, find a locksmith this day and get him to put a lock on my bedroom door."

"Yes, my lady. I would remind my lady she has accepted an invitation to go riding this morning with Lord Frederick. Shall I send a footman with a message canceling the appointment?"

"Why should I want to do that, Kennedy?"

"Because my lord is returned from Paris."

Lucinda had been escorted on many occasions by Lord Freddy Pomfret. He was genial company, safe, and treated her very much as a married lady.

"It makes no difference. My lord can hardly object to an innocent hour's riding with the irreproachable Lord Freddy. Lay out my riding clothes."

By the time Lucinda was cantering along Rotten Row side by side with Lord Freddy, she began to feel very angry indeed. Men who lived lives of dissipation were called rakes. There was a nastier name for women who dared to follow the same course. How would Rockingham like it if he saw *her* in low company?

She reined in her horse and Lord Freddy brought his mount to a halt as well. "Who is the biggest rake in London, Lord Freddy?" she asked.

Lord Freddy thought that Rockingham was by far the biggest, but it would hardly do to voice that opinion aloud. So he thought of the next best—or next worst. Rockingham was dissipated, but one could hardly call him evil. But, thought Lord Freddy, Mr. Dancer, that arbiter of fashion, that fabulously wealthy man, was surely downright evil. He specialized in ruining respectable young ladies and actually seemed to gain more pleasure from their distress and humiliation than from the seductions themselves.

"Mr. Hermes Dancer," he said.

"Ah, and where is this Mr. Dancer to be found?"

"All the *ton* affairs. Good *ton*, but a disgusting lecher. Beg pardon. My wretched tongue," said Lord Freddy turning pink with embarrassment.

"I have been to a few parties," said Lucinda thoughtfully, "but I do not remember anyone of that name."

Despite the duchess's threat, Lucinda had received a great many social invitations since her marriage.

"He has been in Paris like the rest of the world. Now he has returned. He will be at the Bellamys' rout this evening."

Lucinda's brow furrowed in thought and Lord Freddy wondered what she was thinking. Lord Freddy was not yet looking for a wife. He found it comfortable to squire Lucinda around. He liked her old-fashioned ways and how she gravitated, almost by instinct, to the pleasanter and more respectable members of society.

He would have been amazed had he known that Lucinda was seriously considering attracting the attention of Mr. Dancer.

She had become slowly more sophisticated and sure of herself during her husband's absence. She had planned, on his return, to show her gratitude to him by being a meek and complacent wife. She had shyly hoped he would approve of the redecoration of his home. But his drunken embrace of the night before had not revolted her. Far from it. He *had* smelled of sweat and drink, but not offensively so. His touch had started a fire in her body. She had found herself in that moment yearning for his embrace, and that was what had made her desperate mind find exactly the right words to repulse him. When Rockingham kissed her, she wanted him to be sober. More than that—she wanted him to be in love with her. The thought of his mistress, Maria Deauville, burned in her mind. Lucinda did not yet know that what she felt for Maria Deauville was a burning hate caused by jealousy. All she knew was that she wanted revenge on the marquess. She wanted to see if he could be made jealous.

Benson, who had been left behind in London to continue her spying while her mistress, Mrs. Deauville, went to Paris, was lingering outside in Berkeley Square when Kennedy emerged to go to the shops to buy her mistress some ribbons.

Kennedy did not know she was betraying her mistress to an enemy by gossiping to Benson. She did not know of Maria Deauville's reputation or her connection with the marquess. Benson had led Kennedy to believe that she worked for a correct and elderly lady. Convinced that Benson was as discreet and loyal as she was herself, Kennedy felt free to gossip.

Benson quickly joined her and persuaded her to go to a pastry cook's for lemonade before continuing on her shopping expedition.

As soon as the two ladies' maids were seated in the pastry cook's, Kennedy told Benson of the marquess's arrival home. "My lady has told me to put a lock on her bedroom door," she said. "I am going on to the locksmith's directly I purchase the ribbons."

"But surely it isn't natural for a wife to remain a virgin," exclaimed Benson.

"It's not for us to query the ways of our

betters," said Kennedy primly. Then she relented. "But I tell you, Benson, with the master being so drunk and him coming back with a lot of doxies, it stands to reason the mistress wouldn't want anything to do with him."

Benson carefully treasured up this gossip. She had been told to report to Mr. Carter in Mrs. Deauville's absence.

And so, in his turn, Mr. Carter learned of Rockingham's noisy return home and of the request for a lock on the bedroom door.

He thought quickly. He would like to see the Rockinghams together, but, frightened of his cousin's tricky temper, did not want to call at Berkeley Square. "Where do the Rockingham's go today?" he asked Benson.

"Kennedy said her mistress was to go to a rout at the Bellamys'."

"Splendid," said Mr. Carter, ignoring Benson's hopefully outstretched hand. The maid was paid enough by Maria. He had no intention of wasting any of his money on a mere servant.

7

CHUMLEY LAY IN BED while Lucinda was out riding, luxurating in the feel of lavender-scented sheets and enjoying the ministrations of the pretty little housemaid who appeared to open his curtains and present him with a steaming cup of chocolate.

The marquess would soon ruin it all. Chumley was sure of that. Then it would be back to living in a cold, dirty, servantless house. Chumley sipped his chocolate and thought about his new mistress. It was a pity she could not be spared the inevitable. Now, the marquess, Chumley reflected, always behaved badly in town. On his travels and adventures, on the other hand, he lived frugally and healthily. Except Paris, of course, thought Chumley with a shudder. Then, when he traveled to his estates in Wiltshire, he lived a quiet life there. He was a good landlord and no one who knew the Savage Marquess of London would recognize the hardworking lord of the country estates who attended meticulously to his tenants' wants and drank water with his meals.

A devil in town and an angel in the country, mused Chumley. Perhaps for the gentle marchioness's sake, it might be well to see if he could prompt his master into taking a visit to Cramley, his country home, where the rooms were always clean and airy and the servants remained the same.

My lady had done well with her choice of servants, thought Chumley, except perhaps for the lady's maid, who looked like a large rawboned mare. Ladies' maids, in Chumley's opinion, should be neat, small-boned, and French. He heard his master beginning to stir in the next room and hoped the marquess would not call for another bath. He got out of bed and dressed and then went down to the kitchens to order the marquess's breakfast.

The Marquess of Rockingham arrived at the breakfast table an hour later. He had to ask Chumley where he could now expect to find his breakfast. Before, he had eaten it served on a battered desk in a gloomy study at the back of the hall. But the little morning room, next to the drawing room on the second floor, had been refurbished. The marquess eyed the primrose silk upholstery of the new furniture and the primrose silk curtains at the sunny windows and wondered for the first time how much all this redecoration was costing him.

"Where is my lady?" he asked Humphrey as the butler slid a plate of steak and mushrooms in front of him and filled a tankard with small beer.

"My lady is out riding."

"Alone?"

"No, my lord. I believe my lady is escorted by Lord Frederick Pomfret."

"Well, she won't come to any harm there," said the marquess, opening a copy of *The Times*, which had been ironed so that he would not get his fingers stained with ink.

"I think I hear my lady arriving back," said Humphrey.

"Good. Fetch her in."

After a few moments, his wife entered the room. He put down the paper and looked at her. She was wearing a dashing green velvet riding dress with gold frogs, and a mannish riding hat was rakishly balanced on her curls.

"Sit down, Lucinda," said the marquess. "Had breakfast?"

"No, Rockingham."

"Good. You may join me. Now, tell me how much of my money you have managed to get through since my departure?"

"I have all the bills in my room, Rockingham, but I would say about eight hundred pounds."

"And your new wardrobe?"

"That is included in the price."

"Come, my sweeting, stop funning. The furniture is of the first stare, the whole house has been rewallpapered and painted, and your clothes are expensively cut."

Lucinda removed her hat and shook out her curls. "It is like this, Rockingham," she said. "The servants and I painted and wallpapered the rooms ourselves. The furniture is not Sheraton or Chippendale but is made by an excellent but unknown craftsman in Islington. My clothes come from a dressmaker in Whitechapel, Mrs. Meyer, a German lady. I met her by chance when I was in an East End warehouse choosing paint—it is so much cheaper there than in the West End, you know—and we fell to talking, and she told me she could make clothes as well as any famous London dressmaker but could not afford a good address and so I decided to patronize her. She is quite brilliant. I have only to show her an illustration in, say, *La Belle Assemblée*, then she can copy it and yet add an individual touch to it."

"And how did you manage to find this warehouse with cheap paint?"

"Ah, that was easy. A poor section of the town does not charge the same high prices for goods as an expensive quarter, and so I went to the poor. As you can see, Rockingham, it is just the same quality as you will find in your friends' houses. In fact, probably the most expensive item I bought was a closed stove for the kitchen."

"I did not know I had married an astute businesswoman," he said with a laugh.

Lucinda looked at the laughter in his green eyes, at the strength of his handsome face, and then at his long, slim hands. Her heart beat at a suffocating rate and she looked away.

Humphrey served Lucinda with her usual breakfast of toast and tea and then left the room.

The marquess picked up his knife and fork and continued to eat with all the signs of a hearty appetite.

His wife surveyed him with growing irritation. He showed absolutely no recollection of the events of the night before.

"Is it going to be your habit, Rockingham, to descend on me with parties of rowdy drunken friends and Cyprians?"

"To what are you referring?"

"To the events of last night."

"What happened last night?" the marquess asked with all the conscienceless air of one who usually forgets the episodes of the previous evening and thinks all the world behaves in the same way.

"You came back here from Paris

accompanied by the dregs of humanity. When you had sent them packing, or rather, Chumley had, you then mounted to my bedchamber and attempted to assault me."

"Was I successful?" the marquess asked curiously.

"No."

"Then why are you looking so nasty? You agreed not to interfere with my way of life."

"I cannot stop you from turning your own home into a bear garden," said Lucinda. "I can, however, attempt to keep you to your promise to leave me alone for six months."

The marquess put down his knife and fork and regarded his wife in haughty amazement.

"Are you daring to tell me what I should or should not do?"

"I am merely reminding you of your promise."

"Very well," the marquess shouted. "You have my promise, you whey-faced Methodist. Get out of here and do not dare to spoil my breakfast by moralizing again."

"I am not finished my own breakfast," Lucinda said, trying to stand her ground, although her voice shook.

The marquess stood up, went around the table, picked up her plate of toast and cup of tea, and threw them both in the fireplace.

"Now you have," he grated. " Get out!"

Lucinda fled.

Kennedy returned from her shopping expedition to tell Lucinda the locksmith would be arriving within the hour and found her mistress, facedown on her bed, crying her eyes out. Kennedy clucked and exclaimed and went down to the kitchens to fetch Lucinda a restorative cup of tea, where she heard about the shouting from the morning room and how my lady's breakfast had been found among smashed china on the hearth. Kennedy was very fond of her young mistress but found with a twinge of unease that she was gleefully saving up all this dramatic gossip to relay to Benson. Benson was so interested, so sympathetic, and surely so discreet, that it was a pleasure to unburden herself. The lady's maid was about to leave the kitchen with the tea when Humphrey added with a shake of his head, "It's a strange marriage. I was waiting outside the door of the morning room in case I was called, and I couldn't help hearing what they were saying. Seems the mistress got my lord to agree not to touch her for a sixmonth."

Kennedy's eyes widened in amazement. All thought of discretion was gone. This was too good a piece of gossip to keep to herself.

Lucinda drove out that afternoon to make

calls on a few of the new friends she had made.

The Marquess of Rockingham heard her go but made no move to stop her. He fortunately did not know of the new lock on Lucinda's bedroom door, for the servants, fearing his wrath, had smuggled the locksmith up the back stairs.

For the moment, the odd restless feeling which usually plagued him had left him. He admitted reluctantly that it had a lot to do with the calm and pleasant atmosphere created by the new furnishings. He decided to have a relaxed afternoon at home, reading a book.

He settled down in the saloon after having taken a look in his study. That had not been touched by the decorators. It looked as gloomy as a prison cell. The marquess sipped tea and idly followed the text of the book, giving it only half his attention. It would be quite jolly, he thought, perhaps to have a simple meal at home, talk to Lucinda, and go to bed early. Then he wondered whether she had any engagements. He looked at the card rack on the mantel and then rose to have a closer look. That was when he heard Humphrey opening the door to a visitor. The marquess frowned. He should have told the butler that he was not at home to anyone and so have a peaceful few hours.

"The Duchess of Barnshire," announced Humphrey gloomily.

The marquess swung about, his expression guarded and withdrawn. "Good day, Mother," he said. "I have no doubt you have called to berate me about my marriage."

"Of course," said the duchess. "Of all the follies you have committed, Rockingham, this is the worst."

The marquess wondered illogically whether his mother had ever called him by his first name. "Sit down, Mother," he said. "Do not excercize yourself too much over a matter which does not concern you."

"You should have asked our permission," raged his mother. Her eyes were green, but unlike her son's, of a paler color. Her carefully dressed black hair under a turban of purple velvet showed streaks of gray. Her face, weather-beaten from many hours on the hunting field, was harsh and masculine.

"I must remind you I am not a minor," the the marquess said. "Nor can you indulge in any of your favorite disciplines like having me stripped naked and beaten in front of the servants or locked in a closet without food for two days."

"Tish! Do you still hold that against me? All children are disciplined thus. Wait until you have children of your own. The lash of the whip never did you any harm."

A picture of the small, terrified, oversensitive child he had once been rose before the marquess's eyes.

"Let me make one thing clear," he said. "My marriage is my business and I will not stand criticism of my wife."

"Even a wife who removes my portrait and says it is because she did not like it? Even a wife who had me shown out before my call was over?"

"She did that?" exclaimed the marquess.

"Yes. And she had obviously been doing the housework herself."

A slow smile crossed the marquess's face. For the first time, a genuine glow of admiration for Lucinda spread through his mind.

"I am glad she managed to find another place for that portrait of you, Mother," he said. "Although I admit it does you justice, from the hard lines of your face to the nasty little smile on your mouth."

His mother rose, and before he could guess what she meant to do, she had delivered a backhanded slap across his cheek. One of her many rings cut a jagged scratch.

He rang the bell. "Humphrey," he said quietly, "show her grace out and make sure she never sets foot in this house again."

"You will be sorry for this insolence," said his mother. "Very sorry."

The marquess stood still after she had left. Then he took out a handkerchief and dabbed at the cut on his cheek. He noticed his hand was trembling slightly, and swore.

Gone was the peace of the day. He was in London, and London was full of pleasures and amusements. He called for his carriage and summoned Chumley and told him to be ready to accompany him. And Chumley, seeing the hectic gleam in his master's eyes, cursed the Duchess of Barnshire under his breath. The valet knew another long day and night of dissipation lay ahead.

"Why, Miss Benson!" exclaimed Kennedy as she turned into Berkeley Square, carrying a bottle of magic fluid which was supposed to remove all stains. She had discovered a small splash of wine on Lucinda's blue silk gown, had read an advertisement for Johnson's Patent Stain Remover in the *Morning Post*, and had gone to the Haymarket to buy some.

"I was out walking," said Benson, "and hoped to see you, Miss Kennedy."

"You do seem to have a great deal of free time," said Kennedy.

"You forget, my mistress is abroad," said Benson, "and the fact is, I am mortal worried because she did not take me with her. What if she returns with one of them Frenchies and I lose my lob?"

Kennedy was immediately sympathetic, as Benson knew she would be, and so Kennedy was easily persuaded to walk a little way to a pastry cook's. A warning bell was sounding in Kennedy's head, telling her not to be indiscreet. But poor Benson was so worried about her job, and was such a good and comforting friend, that Kennedy soon found herself telling the sympathetic Benson about Lucinda's marriage.

Cleverly, Benson extracted every last mite of information.

After she left Kennedy, she hurried to Mr. Zeus Carter's lodgings. That gentleman was lying in his bed, having suffered a bad fall down his own staircase by trying to make the descent earlier that day in all the glory of fixed spurs. One of the sharp spurs had dug itself into the woodwork of the stairs and Mr. Carter had fallen heavily and twisted his ankle.

Benson was ushered into the darkened bedchamber. "I hope you have brought good news," said Mr. Carter faintly.

The lady's maid approached the bed. "I bring very good news," she said.

"Well, well, out with it."

"Such good news deserves a reward."

"What!" Mr. Carter struggled up against the pillows, groped for his quizzing glass on the bedside table, raised it to one eye, and stared at Benson.

"I said, sir, that such good news deserves a reward."

"Nonsense. Take yourself off. Mrs. Deauville shall learn of your impertinence. You will lose your job."

"My mistress does not have much of a reputation," said Benson, "but she would have less were I ever to open my mouth. I am sure Lord Rockingham might be interested to learn that while he was paying her keep she was consorting with Mr. Dancer."

"You would not—"

"*And*," went on Benson, "I am also sure the Marchioness of Rockingham would be vastly interested to learn that part of my duties are to spy on her."

Mr. Carter regarded her with hate.

"How much?"

"Ten guineas."

"*Ten guineas!*" screeched Mr. Carter. "You wicked woman. That is a fortune."

Benson stood before him, hands demurely folded.

"Oh, very well," he said finally. He paid her the money and then listened eagerly to the news.

"You have done well," he said when she had finished. "Oh, I wish Maria would return from Paris."

When Benson had left, Mr. Carter decided that he must be brave and rouse himself that evening to go to the Bellamys' rout. If there was any love between Rockingham and Lucinda, he would spot it. But if there were none there, then he, Zeus Carter, had nearly five months left of that six-month bargain to make mischief.

He was about to sink back into the sleep that had been disturbed by Benson's visit when his valet announced that Mrs. Deauville was desirous of seeing him.

"Show her up," cried Mr. Carter. He could hardly wait to tell Maria all his news.

Maria Deauville had left Paris in pursuit of the marquess, but the ridgepole of her carriage had broken on the route to Dieppe and she had been delayed three days waiting for it to be repaired, so that although the marquess had been held back two days at Dieppe, she found herself still a day behind him on the chase to London.

She felt bitterly that Rockingham had cheated her out of a wedding. Maria knew herself to be good *ton*. Her reputation was, perhaps, a trifle cracked, but of all the marquess's mistresses, she was the one who had lasted longest. He had once confided in her his desire for children and she had considered that tantamount to a proposal. She had been proud that she was the only woman who appeared to be able to control his wild moods. She listened with growing excitement to Mr. Carter's news. But then, at the end of it, he told her pettishly of Benson's demand for money.

"You did not give her any—of course," said Maria.

"I had to!" said Mr. Carter. "Why, she said an I did not, for a start she would tell Rockingham that you had been, um, *entertaining* Mr. Dancer during his absences, and that, for a second hit, she would tell his wife that she was being ordered to spy on her."

"You numbskull," hissed Maria. "Do you not see she has tasted blood, and will soon want more—and more—and then in the end she will go to Rockingham. Did we not agree that servants should not be bribed, for bribed servants are greedy and treacherous?"

"You left me alone with the problem." Mr. Carter sulked. "I cannot think of everything. I am already doing enough. I have twisted my ankle, yet I am prepared to rouse myself from my sickbed to go to the Bellamys' rout this evening so that I may observe the Rockinghams together. If there is no love there, then we have plenty of time."

"We have no time at all unless I do something about Benson," Maria snarled. "Oh, go back to sleep, you milksop. I came straight here before going home. Can I expect to find my maid there?"

"I suppose so," Mr. Carter mumbled, pulling the blankets up to his chin. "Do not look so fierce, Mrs. Deauville. You see before you a grievously injured man who is yet prepared to pull his poor tortured body from this bed to venture out this evening on your behalf."

"And on your own, my dear friend. If you are trying to make me believe you have forgot for one moment that you are Rockingham's heir, then you are an even greater fool than I believe you to be."

This was too much for Mr. Carter. He pulled the blankets right over his head and waited until he heard the light patter of her feet descending the stairs.

Benson was relieved that her mistress showed no signs of having visited Mr. Carter, and no signs of making preparations to do so. Maria told her maid she had just returned from Paris, and there was nothing in her manner to show she knew of the maid's black-mail. Benson knew a horrendous scene would descend on her the minute Mrs. Deauville *did* find out, but it was pleasant not to have to face up to it right away.

She busied herself therefore in preparing her mistress's bed and lighting a fire in the bedchamber, confident that Mrs. Deauville would wish to sleep after her long journey. But Maria surprised her by saying she was stepping out again for a few moments.

But she was gone for almost an hour and, on her return, she appeared very excited and told Benson that they were to go a little out of town to a certain inn where they would meet a man who had intelligence which would ruin Lucinda in the eyes of her husband.

Benson was ordered to make ready to go with her mistress.

"The fellow is demanding a great deal of money in small coin," said Maria. "Put this money belt around your waist and keep it safe."

The maid gasped at the weight of the belt. "It's so heavy, madam, I don't know that I can stand."

"You will be traveling in a carriage, not walking," Maria snapped.

Benson was thin and slight and middle-aged. But she was tough and wiry and soon became accustomed to the heavy weight about her middle.

She became increasingly elated as the carriage bore them out of London. If Mrs. Deauville was prepared to pay such a large sum—for, small coinage or not, the terrible weight still meant quite a bit of money—then surely she would pay up handsomely to her, Benson, as well.

The carriage finally halted on Maria's instructions in the courtyard of a quiet country inn a little way from the main Richmond road. The day was fine and Maria asked the landlord to bring them glasses of ratafia out-of-doors.

There was a pretty garden at the back of the inn beside a lily pond. Maria ordered the table and chairs to be moved into the sun, then into the shade, and then finally placed at the edge of the water.

Glad this exquisite customer had finally made up her mind, and reminding himself to keep checking on her in case she wanted anything further, for the table was now placed out of sight of the windows of the inn, the landlord beat a thankful retreat.

"Oh dear," Maria exclaimed, "I have left my stole in the carriage and it is become a little chilly."

"Would you not care to remove to inside the inn?" Benson asked.

"No, no, silly woman. I went to all this trouble because I desire secrecy when this fellow arrives. In fact, as you pass through the inn, tell the landlord not to appear again until I send for him."

"Very good, madam." Benson went off to carry out her instructions and, as she did so, the maid could not help wondering about the character of the man who was coming to sell news of Lady Rockingham. Would he be clever and wise like herself, or merely a low cunning person? Perhaps he might be the sort of man with whom she could join forces. Benson was well and truly wrapped up in this rosy fantasy by the time she returned with her mistress's stole.

She stood to attention behind Maria's chair.

"No, you may be seated," said Maria. "You will observe I ordered ratafia for you as well."

"Very good of you, madam," said Benson, sitting down on a chair with her back to the pond.

"In Paris," said Maria with a little laugh, "the maids can drain off a little glass like this in one gulp. Can you do the same, Benson?"

"Oh, easily, madam," said Benson, tossing the contents down her throat.

Odd's fish, will she never die? thought Maria impatiently as the effects of the arsenic she had put in her maid's drink took violent effect. How she does gargle and choke and drum her heels on the grass! I hope she does not alert the landlord.

But Benson at last lay still, conveniently at

the edge of the pond. Maria stooped and rolled the body in. The pond, as she knew from a previous visit, was deep and weedy. The lifeless body, weighted down with the heavy money belt which Maria had filled with lead, sank down into the murky, opaque green depths of the pond. A few ripples spread out. A duck put its head on one side and surveyed Maria with such a comic expression of surprise that she nearly laughed aloud.

Then she sat down and finished her own drink after rinsing out Benson's glass in the pond.

Then she went into the inn and paid for the drinks, asking the landlord if he had seen anything of her maid. When he said he had not, she replied that the silly woman must already be in the carriage. She then went out to the carriage and told the coachman that Benson had looked most peculiar and appeared to have run away. What was the reason for it? Had Benson been up to anything? The coachman shook his head and said she had gone out and about a lot while the mistress was in Paris.

On her return, Maria conveniently found a diamond necklace missing and raised the alarm. Her butler suggested calling the Runners but Maria wept pathetically and said the scandal would be too much for her to bear.

As ladies' maids were the most unpopular creatures next to governesses in any household, since they had to be waited on by the servants just as if they were the aristocracy, the other members of Maria's staff were gleefully prepared to believe the worst of Benson.

The maid had never talked of any family, had never seemed to have either friends or relations. Maria was confident that she would soon be forgotten.

And as Benson's still body moved sluggishly to and fro in the depths of the inn pond, Maria Deauville, resplendent in agates and a gown of gold tissue, set out for the Bellamys' rout.

8

THE BELLAMYS' HOME WAS in Chelsea, which was considered to have the advantages of being nearly in the country without being too vulgarly isolated from the center of the town.

Beside Lucinda in the carriage sat Kennedy, the maid, hoping that Benson might be there. Kennedy often accompanied her mistress to various *ton* affairs, but so far Benson, and her mistress, had been absent from them all. But if this Mrs. Deauville were indeed such an elderly lady and addicted to travel, then it surely followed that she would not be in the habit of attending the same functions as the Marchioness of Rockingham.

Lucinda had waited and waited, hoping that her husband would return and escort her. She had chided herself during the day on her lack of courage in fleeing when he had smashed her breakfast. And of what good would it be to flirt with this Mr. Dancer if Rockingham were not there to see it?

Lucinda's dress had been hurriedly altered

by Mrs. Meyer at the last minute to turn it into a bolder style than she usually wore. It was of green-and-white-striped silk, cut in the French manner—that is, in a simple demure style which nonetheless managed to show off a great deal of her figure. Mrs. Meyer had said cynically that French designers were a miracle of how to make a lady appear seductive without making her look like a demirep.

The Bellamys' house was a pleasant Queen Anne mansion surrounded by a high wall. As was the custom when giving a rout, all the curtains were drawn back and there was a blaze of light from top to bottom.

Lucinda was no longer afraid of these social affairs. She had made a few friends, enough to guarantee she had someone to talk to. She felt she did not belong in London society and therefore treated all their peculiar shibboleths and taboos with all the wary respect of an intelligent explorer staying with a curious, slightly dangerous, and primitive tribe.

As Kennedy arranged Lucinda's dress in the anteroom reserved for the ladies and pinned up some stray tendrils which had come loose from underneath her mistress's headdress of twined vine leaves and seed pearls, Lucinda once more found herself surrounded by ladies anxious to find out the name of her dressmaker. Lucinda was feminine enough to want to keep the name of this treasure to herself, but, on the other hand, she was very much her father's daughter, and so she gave out Mrs. Meyer's direction. There were many flutterings and exclamations of *"Whitechapel!"* as if Lucinda had said Mrs. Meyer were in Labrador instead of the East End of London.

Lucinda and Kennedy then lined up on the staircase, inching up slowly a little bit at a time. A rout was a peculiar affair. The people were the only entertainment. Neither dancing, nor refreshments, nor cards was supplied. About half an hour was spent trying to get into the saloon where one's host held court, half an hour of socializing, then another half hour fighting out, and then at least an hour waiting on the step while one's coachman battled his way through the press.

At last Lucinda was able to make her curtsy to Lord and Lady Bellamy. Then she turned to search the overcrowded room for a sign of a familiar face. She saw Lord Freddy and his sister, Agatha, over in a far corner and started to make her way toward them, but glancing all the time from right to left, wondering which of these gentlemen was the famous rake, Mr. Dancer.

Mr. Zeus Carter appeared suddenly in front of her, blocking her way.

He made an elaborate bow and tried to perform his usual flourish with a scented handkerchief, but swiped an angry-looking old lady on the shoulder, who swore at him with all the coarseness of the last century. Mr. Carter shuddered and confined himself to a less dramatic welcome.

"Mr. Carter," said Lucinda. "How do you do?"

"Tolerable, ma'am. Tolerable. Fell downstairs and wrenched my ankle most horribly. In sickbed. Got physician. Said rest. But decided I must attend to pay my respects to you, dear lady."

"I think it would be much more comfortable for you to have stayed in bed and waited until you could call on me at our home instead of in the middle of this sad crush," said Lucinda.

"True. True. But . . . aha, Mrs. Deauville! May I introduce you to the Marchioness of Rockingham."

Deauville. Both Lucinda and Maria stiffened — Lucinda because she knew she was facing Rockingham's mistress; Kennedy because she could hardly believe this fairylike creature could be Benson's employer, Benson who had led her to believe Mrs. Deauville was old.

"May I felicitate you?" said Maria. "One never thought the wild marquess would marry."

"Did one not?" said Lucinda icily, and made to move forward.

But Mr. Carter and Maria stood shoulder to shoulder, blocking her way.

"And where *is* Rockingham?" cooed Maria.

"My husband is about town somewhere," said Lucinda. "He is but recently returned from Paris."

"Ah, yes," said Maria. "I saw him there. Ah, Paris! A city of love and romance."

Lucinda felt sick. It seemed that whenever she tried to rationalize her husband's wild and disgusting behavior, something arose to tell her she could never change him—that she had been a fool to wait this evening, hoping for the return of a man who threw away her breakfast and ordered her from the room.

Although she surveyed Maria with calm, clear eyes, her raging jealous mind was taking in every detail of Maria's dress and appearance. This Mrs. Deauville's gold hair owed nothing to art, and her figure, revealed by a gown of damped gold tissue, was perfect. But her skin owed its seeming purity to a heavy layer of blanc. I hope she dies of lead poisoning, Lucinda thought.

Aloud she said, "You are fortunate indeed, Mrs. Deauville, in finding Paris such a delight.

Other members of the *ton* have informed me it is naught but a medieval sink of vice and filth."

"Perhaps my company cast a rosy glow on my surroundings," said Maria maliciously.

Lucinda took a deep breath and her fine eyes flashed fire. "If, madam," she said in a clear, carrying voice, "you are attempting to tell me you were my husband's mistress before his marriage to me, then I beg you to save your breath. Rockingham's stable of doxies is legendary. I beg you to excuse me."

She forced her way past the spluttering Maria. Mr. Carter let out a nervous titter of laughter and then clamped his hand over his mouth as he saw the rage in Maria's eyes.

"Who is that magnificent creature?" asked a cool voice somewhere above Maria's head.

She looked up and saw the handsome face of Mr. Dancer smiling down at her. She collected herself with an effort and gave a little shrug. " 'Tis Rockingham's new bride. A pert country miss of neither breeding nor background."

"You must introduce me."

"Not I," said Maria. She was about to turn away when she changed her mind and turned back. Rockingham had not seen fit to accompany Lucinda. Would Mr. Dancer's famous charm work with his wife?

"I shall not approach the creature again," she said, "but perhaps Mr. Carter here will do the honors." She flashed a look at Mr. Carter, who rallied and said, "Of course, of course. Follow me."

Lucinda had nearly succeeded in edging her way to Lord Freddy's side when, to her irritation, she once more heard Mr. Carter's drawling, affected voice. "May I present Mr. Dancer?"

Lucinda turned to face the man who she hoped would be instrumental in rousing jealousy in her husband's rakish bosom.

She was pleasurably surprised by what she saw. As with her husband, evil ways and dissipation did not seem to have left their outward mark on Mr. Dancer.

He was tall and broad-shouldered and had a square, pleasant handsome face. His hair was very fair, almost white, and worn somewhat longer than the current fashion, which was for Brutus crops. His eyes were a brilliant blue, dancing and sparkling, and almost hypnotic. He smelled of good soap and fresh linen.

He bowed and took her hand and deposited a light kiss on her glove. "Does your husband attend this evening?" he asked.

"No, alas, I am alone."

"Then I am fortunate. I find your husband a

most terrifying gentleman who would probably call me out were he here."

"And why would he do that?" asked Lucinda, her eyes glinting over her raised fan.

"Your beauty would drive any man mad with jealousy, let alone such a fiery character as Rockingham."

Lucinda sent up a little prayer for forgiveness. "I do not interfere with my husband's life, nor he with mine."

"A very modern marriage," said Mr. Dancer. "Ah, you are already moving away from me. Are you leaving so soon?"

"Yes," said Lucinda. "I do not like routs and do not know why I bothered to attend this one."

"Please accept my escort. I should consider myself honored above all men."

"I should be glad of your company, Mr. Dancer. I need help in pushing my way through this crush."

He led the way and Lucinda followed.

"She is leaving with Dancer," Maria hissed in Mr. Carter's ear. "Dare we hope . . . ?"

"Oh yes," said Mr. Carter. "*Bags* of hope there, I should think."

Mr. Dancer traveled with Lucinda in her carriage. He talked easily and wittily of the plays he had seen. He did not make any bold overtures. Lucinda was surprised to find him such good company. When they arrived in Berkeley Square, she invited him indoors for tea, but Mr. Dancer did not want to risk meeting her husband. Instead, he bowed and begged permission to take her driving on the morrow. Lucinda agreed.

Kennedy followed her mistress into the house. She was very worried. She remembered all the indiscreet gossip she had told Benson. Benson, it had transpired, was not maid to an elderly lady, but to a member of the Fashionable Impure. Kennedy did not know much fashionable gossip, or she would have learned of Mrs. Deauville's reputation, but she prided herself on being able to tell a lady from a demimondaine. And, in Mrs. Deauville she had immediately recognized a demirep. She was desperate to see Benson as soon as possible so that she might demand an explanation.

She prepared her mistress for bed, asking, as she did so, leave to take the following afternoon off. "Of course," Lucinda agreed. "I have been in the habit of dressing myself. Nothing the matter with your family, I trust?"

"My family is well, my lady. They reside in Exeter in Devon, not London. I merely wanted to view the shops."

Lucinda was about to point out that Kennedy had already had more than enough free time to visit as many London shops as she wished, but then she reminded herself of how supportive the maid had been. Possibly Kennedy had a beau, although it was hard to imagine the grim-faced maid being able to attract anybody.

When Kennedy retired, Lucinda found she could not sleep. She lay awake listening for sounds of her husband's return.

She at last fell into a light sleep from which she was roused at three in the morning by the sound of the street knocker. She heard Humphrey going to answer it, her husband's voice, and then the opening and shutting of a downstairs door, possibly the saloon.

This was subsequently followed by a door opening again and her husband roaring some command. Then there was a lot of toing and froing, and then silence. Lucinda shifted uneasily in her bed. Then she got up and locked her bedroom door, realizing she had forgotten to do so. She lay awake for about an hour but there came no sounds of her husband ascending the stairs.

Lucinda remembered the evening she had danced with him at Almack's, remembered the odd feeling of safety she had felt in his arms. She decided to go downstairs to see if she could talk to him, to see if there was anything of worth hiding under that rakish and dissipated exterior.

She rose and pulled on a wrapper over her nightgown, slipped on a pair of flat-heeled shoes, and made her way quietly downstairs. The house was still and silent. Then an old clock in the hall sent out a wheezing volley of chimes, making her start. Holding her bed candle in its flat stick, she pushed open the door of the saloon.

The first thing she saw was a large bath placed before the fire. The marquess had called for a bath, Chumley had grumbled about the work involved carrying it plus cans of water upstairs, and the drunken marquess had cheerfully volunteered to take his bath in the saloon.

The candles were lit so Lucinda blew out her own and made her way forward. How like Rockingham to take his bath, leave towels and soap scattered over the carpet, and then go off to bed without ordering the servants to clean up the mess.

She looked into the bath and found herself staring down at the naked body of her husband.

She let out a stifled little scream and was about to retreat when she realized how still and motionless he was. Only his nose was left above the water. His eyes were closed. He's dead, thought Lucinda. He has finally drunk himself to death.

''Oh, Rockingham!'' she cried. She knelt

down beside the bath and slid her hands under his shoulders and tried to raise him.

Suddenly his heavy eyelids lifted and his green eyes stared straight into her own, the initial dazed look being quickly replaced by one of sheer devilment.

"Hey, this is better," the marquess cried. He seized Lucinda around the waist and tipped her into the bath on top of him and then rolled her down underneath him, pinning her down in the tepid water with his naked body.

"Let me up, you monster!" Lucinda screamed.

Her hair was floating out on the water and she kicked and thrashed impotently under his weight.

"Keep still, damn you!" the marquess shouted, forcing his lips down on hers so that her head went under and the kiss took place underwater. Lucinda surfaced from his embrace, gasping and spluttering.

"My lord?" came a voice from the doorway.

"Chumley! Thank heaven!" said Lucinda.

"What the deuce do you mean by crashing in here?" demanded the marquess.

"I heard your lordship roar," said the unperturbable Chumley. "But as my services are obviously not required—"

"No, they are not, curse your eyes."

"Wait!" screamed Lucinda. She succeeded in struggling out from under her husband's body by fighting and kicking. The marquess tried to pin her down again. The bath tipped over and naked marquess and dripping marchioness rolled over the carpet. Sobbing with shame and outrage, water pouring from her, Lucinda fled from the room.

"Gone away!" cried the marquess, setting off in pursuit. But he tripped over something and fell in the hall. He whipped about, suspecting Chumley had stuck out his foot, but the valet was standing with his arms folded, looking at the ceiling. The marquess leapt to his feet and shot off up the stairs after his wife.

Lucinda ran into her room, remembered she must lock the door, and was just about to do so when the door crashed open and her naked and grinning husband stood on the threshold.

Lucinda seized a warming pan that was propped on the end of the bed and, holding it like a broadsword with both hands, she swung it around and let it fly, straight at her husband. He ducked and darted back into the corridor. Lucinda fell against the door, slamming it shut and turning the key in the lock.

There came a furious kicking and pounding at the door.

"Your dressing gown, my lord." Chumley's voice came faintly to Lucinda's ears.

"Who put this lock on the door?" the marquess shouted.

"Possibly you did so yourself," Chumley said. "I think there always was a lock on this particular door. A letter came today from Mr. Rendell, one of your tenant farmers. It appears he is going to shoot Mr. Kay, one of your other tenant farmers, over a matter of boundary rights." Chumley was expected to open and read all his master's post.

"I know them both well. What am I supposed to do about it in the middle of the night?"

"It is nearly morning and we set out for the country in a few hours, which is why I brought up the matter of the farmers' dispute."

"Chumley, I do not recall making arrangements to go to the country. When did I tell you?"

"Why, the night, my lord, when we were returned from Paris."

"Can't remember anything about last night."

"Exactly, my lord."

There was a long silence. Inside the bedroom, Lucinda waited, trembling.

Then she heard her lord say in a puzzled

voice, "What am I doing standing in this corridor dripping wet?"

"You walked in your sleep, my lord. If you will come this way, I will proceed to barber you. You will agree, my lord, that since you have already had a good night's sleep, there is no reason to delay our departure."

Lucinda let out a slow breath of relief as she heard their footsteps going away.

She pulled off her wet nightclothes, toweled herself dry, and put on a fresh nightdress. She was just about to get into bed when there came a scratching at the door.

"Who is it?" she called sharply.

"Chumley, my lady."

"Are you alone?"

"Yes, my lady."

Lucinda slid out of bed and crossed the room and unlocked the door.

She stood on tiptoe and peered over Chumley's shoulder as if expecting to find her husband crouched behind his valet.

"I am no Trojan horse, my lady," said Chumley in hurt accents.

Despite the upheaval of her emotions, Lucinda began to giggle. "A Trojan horse carries the enemy inside, Chumley. Come in and state your business. But first: can I expect another visit from my lord?"

"No, my lady. He is now convinced he has

enjoyed a good night's sleep and we are about to set out for his country home."

"He is surely mad!"

"No, my lady. Like most of our *ton*-nish gentlemen, my lord cannot remember anything that happens when he is drunk."

"So it was you who persuaded him that he had made arrangements to leave?"

"In a manner of speaking, my lady. I am accustomed to anticipating my master's wishes."

"And you are about to anticipate another, which is why you are here?"

"Yes, my lady. I think my lord would like the direction of Lord Chamfreys."

"Why, pray?"

"To call on Mr. Westerville. It is only fitting that he should pay his respects to his father-in-law."

"A most worthy thought, Chumley, but spare my poor sick father such a visitation."

Chumley stared up at the cornice as if it were the most fascinating thing he had ever seen.

"My lord is very quiet and hardworking in the country," the valet said. "He drinks only water and attends to matters of the estate. Much better to have such a visit over and done with, my lady, then to risk Mr. Westerville's paying a surprise visit to town."

"Very well," Lucinda said reluctantly.

"Wait until I write a letter to my father."

Chumley cast an anxious look in the direction of the door. "Perhaps just the address will do, my lady. My lord may come in search of me."

Lucinda hurriedly scrawled down the address and handed it to him. Chumley scurried off.

I wish I could go to the country with him to see this husband of mine in a virtuous mood, Lucinda thought wistfully, and then immediately scolded herself for being a fool. Rockingham was a monster. She wanted to see how *he* would like being married to a philanderer. And what would he say if *she* behaved like him, roaring and shouting and smashing things?

Then she remembered her engagement with Mr. Dancer. She wondered whether to cancel it now that Rockingham was not going to be about to be made jealous—if he could be made jealous.

But perhaps it would be as well to lay a little grondwork. She could not turn into a rake overnight. But women were not called rakes; they were called sluts and worse names. Lucinda thought of Mrs. Deauville and her face hardened. Society could call her any name it pleased just so long as her infuriating husband received a taste of his own medicine.

9

Mr. Dancer had no thought of seducing Lucinda as he set out to take her for a drive. Although he was physically well-built, it was vanity which made him keep his body trim rather than any desire to excel in manly sports. Rockingham was too formidable a man to cross and Mr. Dancer had no desire to end up stretched out dead on a dueling field in Chalk Farm or Hampstead Heath.

But he was bored, and the idea of driving Lucinda added a little spice to life. One drive would surely not rouse Rockingham's ire.

As Lucinda climbed into his carriage, he reflected that a great deal of her charm lay in the fact that she was not precisely beautiful by fashionable standards. Her generous mouth seemed made for passion and he found the unfashionable slenderness of her body enchanting. For although Lucinda had put on some much-needed weight, she was still considered too thin in an age that appreciated large bosoms and plump, rounded arms.

He had to confess that Lucinda's seemingly artless statement that her husband was gone from town did ease a certain trepidation in his breast.

The day was fine and warm although a mass of black clouds piling up in the west did not augur well for the rest of the day.

Everything in the park was very still and bright. Trees were emerald green, and masses of roses in the flowerbeds by the Serpentine a gaudy blaze of pink and white.

"And how does married life go with you?" asked Mr. Dancer.

"I do not know yet," said Lucinda. "I do not see much of my husband." Then she remembered his naked body stretched out in the bath and a deep blush suffused her face.

"Ah, well, there is great freedom in London society for a married woman," said Mr. Dancer.

"I do not think women have much freedom," Lucinda said. "Even being rich appears to mean one is locked in a cage of idleness, and it does not suit me to be idle."

"Most ladies have their amours."

"They are welcome to them," said Lucinda, forgetting she was supposed to be attracting Mr. Dancer. "You see, I should think that to have an affair would involve a tedious amount of intrigue and dread."

"But if the heart is engaged, why then it can be heaven!"

"I do not think infidelity is considered one of the qualities necessary to get through the pearly gates."

"Ah, a Puritan."

"Not I," said Lucinda. "How well you drive, Mr. Dancer."

"I am reputed to be quite good," he said. "Of course, I could not hope to outclass your husband."

A strong feeling of resentment toward her absent husband welled up in Lucinda's breast and she said tartly, "Mr. Dancer, even the respectable Lord Freddy does not drive me in the park to prose on about my husband."

"Pomfret! I have competition for your favors."

"Sir, I did not know you were interested in gaining my favors."

Mr. Dancer had all the practiced seducer's capacity of being able to fall violently in love for a short time. He looked at Lucinda and felt a longing to take her in his arms.

"Why do you frown?" he asked.

"Someone is approaching whom I detest," said Lucinda in a low voice.

Mr. Dancer looked with interest at the advancing carriage and recognized the occupants as the Countess of Clifton and her daughter, Lady Ismene. As both carriages came abreast, Mr. Dancer bowed but Lucinda dipped her parasol to hide her face.

"Did you see that, Mama!" exclaimed Ismene, twisting her head around to look back at Mr. Dancer's retreating carriage. "That slut, Lucinda! Not content with marrying one rake, she must needs take another as lover."

"It is a brave man who would risk Rockingham's displeasure," said the countess. "Either Mr. Dancer is deeply in love at last or Rockingham is gone from town."

When Lady Clifton and Ismene returned home, Ismene sent her new maid around to Berkeley Square to see if anything could be found out about the whereabouts of Rockingham. The maid returned after a while to say that a kitchen maid had said my lord was in the country at Cramley, his home in Wiltshire.

"Then he shall hear from me how she behaves in his absence," said Ismene. "Wait there, and I shall give you a letter for the post."

Lucinda returned home after a pleasant drive. But she had no interest in seeing Mr. Dancer again until the presence of her husband should make that necessary.

In vain did Mr. Dancer try to take her to the opera or the theater. Lucinda replied she was much too busy completing the renovations of the house. Had she immediately accepted just one of his invitations, then it is possible that Mr. Dancer's interest in Lucinda would have withered away.

But adversity is a great aphrodisiac and the path of the true philanderer never did run smooth. By the time he reached his own home, Mr. Dancer was convinced he was in love with Lucinda.

Lucinda was surprised to find Kennedy still absent, for it was getting on for six in the evening.

Kennedy had found out Mrs. Deauville's address from Humphrey, the butler, who, unlike Kennedy, knew a great deal of gossip about the *ton.* She had hung about Montague Street, waiting to see if Benson would emerge.

At last she saw a carriage being brought around to the front of the house. Mrs. Deauville came out accompanied by a lady's maid. But this maid was a thick-set middle-aged woman and definitely not Benson.

Waiting until Mrs. Deauville's carriage had turned the corner of the square, Kennedy went forward to the house and made her way down the area steps at the side of the front door.

A kitchen maid answered the door. Kennedy asked for Benson. The kitchen maid looked at Kennedy with disapproval and said, "I shall tell Mr. Quinton you are here."

After a few moments, a butler came to the door and said sharply, "Why do you want to know about Benson?"

"Miss Benson is by way of being a friend of mine," said Kennedy.

"In that case, we don't want your sort around here. Be off with you!"

The door began to close.

Kennedy jammed one of her large feet encased in a serviceable half-boot against the door.

"What do you mean?" she cried. "You must tell me. I am a respectable woman. I am lady's maid to the Marchioness of Rockingham."

The butler thought quickly. Like the rest of Mrs. Deauville's servants, he was well aware of the affair that had gone on between the marquess and Mrs. Deauville. He had also heard of the marquess's marriage and knew that his mistress had gone to Paris in pursuit of Rockingham, only to return alone and in a furious temper.

He made up his mind.

"You had best come in," he said, standing aside and holding open the door.

He led the way into the servants' hall, pulled out a chair for Kennedy, and sat down next to her. "It's like this," Quinton said. "Benson went out driving with Mrs. Deauville the day madam came back from Paris. Mrs. Deauville returned alone and set up an alarm that Benson had stolen a valuable necklace. I suggested calling the Bow Street Runners, but madam wept so bitterly and said she could not bear the scandal."

"Where was Benson last seen?" asked Kennedy.

"At some inn on the Richmond road. She ran away there, the coachman said, although he said it was odd, for he did not see her emerging from the inn."

"And what is the name of this inn?"

"I do not know," said Quinton. "If you are not in league with Benson—and you look like a respectable lady to me—then it is well to leave things as they are."

He leaned closer to Kennedy. "Things have been mortal bad in this house ever since the Marquess of Rockingham got married."

"Why? What has his marriage to do with Mrs. Deauville?"

Quinton looked nervously about and then whispered, "Madam was the mistress o' the marquess—and a mort o' money he spent on her."

"Oh, my poor lady," cried Kennedy, putting her hands up to her hot cheeks.

"Can't see it'll bother her," said the butler

cynically. "These lords always have a bit of pleasure in keeping, married or not."

Kennedy took her leave, determined to forget about Benson. But before she left the street, it hit her that Benson might have been trying to elicit gossip on the instructions of her mistress. What had once seemed like friendly, curious questions from one lady's maid to another now took on a sinister cast. For this ex-mistress had no reason to feel charitable toward the Marchioness of Rockingham.

Kennedy wheeled about and took up a position at the corner of the square, waiting for Mrs. Deauville's return, hoping that lady had only gone out on a call.

A half-hour later, Kennedy saw Mrs. Deauville arrive back, waited until she saw her go inside, and then followed the carriage around to the mews.

The coachman was just heaving himself down from the box when he found Kennedy waiting for him. He watched Kennedy's face curiously as the maid asked for the name of the inn where Benson had disappeared. "I am the Marchioness of Rockingham's lady's maid," ended Kennedy, "and a respectable body."

"It was at the Red Lion, a little way down Wise Road before you gets to Syon Park."

Kennedy thanked him and moved away. She knew she should now return home, but she felt she could not rest without trying to find Benson. Kennedy had become devoted to Lucinda. Her initial desire to find Benson had been to reassure herself that she, Kennedy, had not betrayed Lucinda's trust. Now she felt it was imperative to find Benson, for surely Mrs. Deauville was hatching some plot against Lucinda. If Benson had disappeared at the inn, then it argued that Benson might be found close by. Mrs. Deauville had made no attempt to recover the necklace; therefore it followed that Benson guessed that was the way she would react, and had decamped in an area she already knew.

Thankful that she had money with her, Kennedy hired a post chaise and driver and set out.

Mrs. Deauville was preparing for the evening when her new lady's maid told her that her coachman wanted to see her on an urgent matter.

Curious, Maria told the maid to send the man up.

She listened wide-eyed as the coachman told her of Kennedy's visit. Maria's heart did a somersault. Benson must have betrayed her to this Kennedy and now Kennedy was seeking incriminating evidence.

With a forced little laugh, Maria tossed her coachman a guinea and told him to forget about the matter. But as soon as he had left, she hurriedly dressed and put on a warm cloak, and told her maid she was going off on a discreet visit.

The maid assumed Maria was going to meet some gentleman. Although Maria tried to maintain the manner of a respectable lady of the *ton*, her drawing room was always graced with unattached men or men without their wives.

Like Kennedy, Maria went to a livery stable, but ordered a racing curricle and said she would drive it herself. The owner of the livery stable was so nervous about the fate of his cattle that Maria had to leave a large sum of money with him as security.

She sprang the horses and set out at a breakneck pace in the direction of Richmond.

Many carriages flew past Kennedy's post chaise and so she did not recognize the cloaked figure in the racing curricle when it passed her just as she was approaching Wise Road.

When she got to the inn, Kennedy told the driver of the post chaise to wait. She was about to go toward the inn when the little ostler who had run forward to catch the horses' reins turned and handed her a note. Kennedy carried it over to where a light swung over the courtyard entrance. She read, "Do not go into the inn. Dismiss the carriage and walk back along the road a hundred yards in the easternly direction. Your loving friend, Benson."

Kennedy decided to do as requested. She felt very brave and very intelligent for having guessed that Benson had not gone far from the inn.

She paid the post chaise, wincing at the cost and wondering how she was going to get back to London, for the inn looked too small to boast any rentable carriage and horse at all.

Then she walked down the road in the greenish twilight. It normally did not get dark at that time of year until about ten in the evening, but the black clouds which had threatened all day were slowly covering the whole sky. Far away sounded the low, menacing growl of thunder. Kennedy was just wondering whether she had walked far enough when she heard a faint whinny of horses a little to her left. She stopped, hesitating. But a fugitive Benson would hardly have horses hidden among the trees like a highwayman.

Then a soft voice whispered, "Hist! Over here."

Kennedy looked to the left from where the

voice had come. The bushes and trees by the side of the road were shrouded in approaching night. The road gleamed ahead of her with a metallic sheen. Kennedy had an impulse to take to her heels and run away along that glittering road as fast as she could. The thunder rolled again, nearer this time.

Kennedy took a step toward the bushes. For Lucinda's sake, she must speak to Benson.

She walked boldly into the woods.

The darkness was absolute. Kennedy stopped and listened.

And then those old primitive instincts, so long dormant, told her that Evil stood nearby. Old legends of goblins and witches, heard at her mother's knee, came rushing into Kennedy's frightened mind.

She turned to flee just as a great flash of lightning lit up the sky.

A heavy blow struck her viciously on the back of the head and the maid fell forward on the grass.

Maria Deauville lit a dark lantern and knelt beside the maid. She then took Kennedy by the heels and dragged her through the under-brush until the trees and bushes opened to reveal the dull silver of a winding river.

She rolled the body over and over until it slid into the river. Panting, Maria seized a branch and pushed Kennedy's body out from the shore.

A drop of rain struck her cheek. Why had she not ordered a closed carriage? She could not shelter at the inn, for the landlord would recognize her.

Feeling that life was very unfair, Maria led the horses out from the shelter of the trees onto the road. She picked up the reins and set out for London at breakneck speed. She was lucky. The full force of the deluge held off until she reached Hyde Park turnpike and saw the red-brick front of Apsley House on her left and the red brick of St. George's Hospital on her right.

By the time she had driven the short distance to Manchester Square, she was soaked through. The death of two women did not lie heavily on Maria's soul. They had been servants and their extermination was as justified as the extermination of black beetles in the kitchen. Maria could not bring herself to dispose of Lucinda so easily. Servants and lower orders did not have immortal souls. To murder Lucinda would mean bringing down Divine punishment on her head in the afterlife. Maria did not believe God could punish her while she, Maria, was alive. For Maria had given up praying a long time ago so that God would not know where she was.

The current of the river swept Kennedy out and then back in until her unconscious body bumped against the roots of a weeping willow.

She opened her eyes, struggled, and immediately began to sink. With a great effort she seized the gnarled roots of the tree and pulled herself to dry land.

For a long time she lay facedown. She did not know who she was or where she was.

Half-limping, half-crawling, she made her way away from the river. She came to a road and stumbled along it until she saw the welcoming lights of a small inn.

Mr. Zeus Carter went to the play that evening and, after the performance was over, he called to see Maria in Montague Street. He hoped to speak to her in private, but there were several gentlemen lounging in the drawing room and Mr. Carter knew from experience that they would probably stay for as long as their hostess would let them.

Maria had never looked more beautiful. The shadows of fatigue under her blue eyes made them look enormous and lent her face an appealing air of fragility. It was some time before Mr. Carter began to feel that something was missing. Then he realized that Benson, who usually sat sewing in a corner of the room to give the proceedings a spurious air of respectability, had been replaced by a new maid.

Maria was playing the piano to entertain her guests. When she had finished, Mr. Carter approached the piano and whispered, "Where is Benson? What have you done with her?"

Maria's eyes glittered with a hectic light. "Keep your voice down," she muttered. "Benson is, or was, my affair."

Mr. Carter retreated, baffled. Surely Maria had not sacked Benson. A sacked Benson would be vindictive. The only other way to get rid of Benson and make sure she would not talk would be to . . .

His mind shied away from the thought. The door opened and Mr. Dancer was introduced.

Maria tripped forward to meet him, holding out both her hands.

"And what have you been doing with yourself?" she cried.

"This and that," said Mr. Dancer with a malicious smile. "For one thing, I have been entertaining the new Marchioness of Rockingham."

For a brief moment the smile left Maria's face. Then she said brightly, "You must tell me all about it." She turned and faced the room. "Gentlemen, you all must leave. I have a private matter to discuss with Mr. Dancer."

Mr. Carter rose to leave with the rest.

"Not you," said Maria. "Stay. We shall entertain Mr. Dancer together."

Mr. Dancer leaned against the piano and wondered what Maria was up to.

"Now," Maria said, when her guests had gone, "how did you find the fair marchioness?"

"Delightful. I took her for a drive."

"There is no accounting for taste," said Maria with a shrug. "I would have thought her too provincial to please a man of the world."

"Indeed! And yet Rockingham is more man of the world than I."

"Ah, but perhaps his bride does not please him. They have not yet lain together."

Mr. Dancer studied her face and then turned around and looked slowly at Mr. Carter, who was nervously clicking open and shut a little enameled snuffbox.

"I have it," said Mr. Dancer. "You, my beloved Maria, lost Rockingham to Lucinda, and you, Carter, stand to lose all if the couple have children. You are hoping I will seduce the girl and bring about the ruin of the marriage."

"Nonsense!" cried Mr. Carter, turning pale.

"Fustian," said Maria.

"Pity," Mr. Dancer said, leaning forward and extracing a pinch of snuff from Mr.

Carter's box. "For I am quite prepared to oblige you . . . for a sum, of course."

"How much?" Maria demanded as Mr. Carter babbled protests.

"A trifle. Let me see . . . about five thousand guineas."

"That is an enormous amount of money," said Maria. "And you are rich!"

"I intend to stay rich," said Mr. Dancer, looking amused. "Believe me, I add to my coffers at every opportunity. But perhaps it *is* too much, my sweetest Mrs. Deauville. After all, how can you be sure Rockingham will fall back into your arms were his marriage annulled?"

"Tonight, I feel I can do anything," said Maria, remembering sriking Kennedy down—not with revulsion, but with a feeling of power and exhilaration.

"I wish to be left out of this," said Mr. Carter. "I no longer wish to be a part of it."

"You had better not back out," said Maria. "You are already in this up to your neck."

And Mr. Carter thought of the missing Benson, shuddered, and sat in silence while Mr. Dancer and Maria got down to business.

10

THE MARQUESS OF ROCKINGHAM remained away from London for several weeks. He had received a letter from Lady Ismene telling him of his wife's "affair" with Mr. Dancer. The marquess had been highly amused and had thrown it on the fire. After two weeks, a letter arrived from his mother, telling him pretty much the same thing. He had thrown that missive on the fire too, but he did not laugh. Although he knew his mother to be as dead set on ruining Lucinda's reputation as Ismene, he did begin to think that if he found Lucinda attractive, then it followed that a number of other men must also find her attractive.

But he was convinced that no one would dare to tamper with his property, which is how he thought of his wife. Since he could not lie with her until the six-month period was over, he did not see any reason why he should return to London to court her.

He was surprised, therefore, to find the

peace of his days ruined since the arrival of his mother's letter. He had been laying out flowerbeds at the front of the house. He had never bothered about flowerbeds before, thinking lawns cropped by sheep and bordered by evergreens were garden enough. He had plunged into a frenzy of plans for a laburnun walk, an organgery, a pond, and an herb garden. He was sure Lucinda would like an herb garden.

Chumley saw what his master did not—that all these preparations were being made for Lucinda's homecoming. But the valet held his tongue and prepared himself for a long and peaceful stay in the country.

Then a letter arrived from Lord Freddy Pomfret. It was very long and rambling and full of town gossip and trivia. But at the end of the letter Lord Freddy came to the point. He had tried to tell the Marchioness of Rockingham that Mr. Dancer was not a suitable escort, but for some reason, she would not listen to him.

"I have to go back to town, Chumley," said the marquess. "Did you read this?"

"Of course, my lord. I read all your post."

"And what do you make of it?"

"Mr. Dancer is very amiable and handsome and no doubt my lady is bored and lonely. Before she came to town, she led an active life caring for her father. Time must lie heavy on her hands."

"Let's hope that's the only thing that's lying heavy on her," the marquess said. "We'd better go. Who is going to supervise the workmen and gardeners? There is still much to be done."

"I would suggest Mr. Westerville, my lord. If you do but remember, we removed Mr. Westerville from Lord Chamfreys' home because Mr. Westerville was restored to health. But saint as he is, I do not think he can find the company of such an ignorant man as his vicar amiable."

"You have the right of it. He will be glad of an excuse to retire. This way I can give him more money than he has hithertofore been prepared to accept. We shall call on him, but not a word of his daughter's adventures in town!"

Chumley had been in part right when he had described Lucinda's reasons for letting Mr. Dancer escort her. She had almost forgotten her desire for revenge on her husband. She had, moreover, received a letter from her father praising the marquess to the skies. But she had begun to find Mr. Dancer's admiration of her very seductive. Lucinda, ready to fall in love and ignored by her husband, began to find her heart beating a little faster when Mr. Dancer's tall figure entered the room.

She had also passed her time by making more improvements to the marquess's town house. In between organizing this work and going to balls and parties, she continued to search for Kennedy. Why should the maid disappear and leave all her belongings behind?

Lucinda had not engaged the services of another maid, always hoping to hear word from Kennedy. She finally placed an advertisement in the *Morning Post*, offering a reward for news of the missing lady's maid.

She returned to Berkeley Square after placing the advertisement, to find a letter from her husband waiting for her. It was very short, very curt, and to the point. He would be returning on the seventh and expected her to be at home to receive him. Lucinda's hand, holding the letter, began to shake. That very day was the seventh, and she was engaged to go to the opera with Mr. Dancer.

Lucinda crushed the letter in her hand. Why should she stay at home for his arrival? He would probably be drunk and offensive.

To her relief, by the time she left for the opera, Rockingham had still not put in an appearance. She tried to forget about him, but finally, during the interval, found herself blurting out the news of his return.

Mr. Dancer thought furiously. He had been taking things very easily, noticing the increasing glow of welcome in Lucinda's eyes. He must move very quickly. He wondered if Rockingham had heard of his courtship of his wife.

"You are very pale," he said sympathetically. "Will he rage at you?"

Mr. Westerville's daughter had a conscience which told her she should not be discussing her husband with anyone, but Lucinda felt frightened and very alone. "I am sure he will," she said. "But he is my husband, after all, and I must learn to put up with it."

"Were you my wife," Mr. Dancer said in an intense voice, "then I would cherish you."

"Do not speak thus," Lucinda said breathlessly. "You should not."

"I cannot bear to see you suffer. The man is a monster—a libertine."

"Such has been said about you yourself."

"Alas, my poor reputation. And yet my feelings for you are pure. If I were as black as I have been painted, would I have held my passions in check for so long? I respect you and I love you."

"Mr. Dancer!" cried Lucinda, tears starting to her eyes. "I did not guess for a moment your feelings were seriously engaged."

"Do not stay with Rockingham. Run away with me."

"No," Lucinda said. "That I cannot do."

"Then promise me if you need me, you will send word to me."

"Yes, I promise. Now, do not let us talk about such painful things. Look! The opera is about to begin again."

When Mr. Dancer's carriage rolled into Berkeley Square later that night, the Marquess of Rockingham's house was a blaze of lights. The curtains of the downstairs saloon were drawn back and a tall figure could be seen pacing up and down.

"I had better set you down here rather than take you to the door," said Mr. Dancer nervously. "He may challenge me to a duel, and I would not have his blood on my hands."

Lucinda was set down on the opposite side of the square. Just as she was approaching the house, the marquess's broad shoulders blotted out the light in the saloon and his face was pressed against the glass.

He saw her approach, and by the time Lucinda was walking up the front steps, he had the door open and was standing there with his arms folded.

"Well, madam wife?" he demanded.

Lucinda pushed past him and went into the

saloon. "Faith, I am tired," she said, sinking into a chair and kicking off her shoes.

"Did you not get my letter?" he shouted, striding into the room and glaring down at her.

"Oh, that," Lucinda said. " Well, sir, as you see, the house was ready for your return and the servants waiting."

"But not you!"

"What a tedious bore you are, Rockingham," sighed Lucinda. ' 'It has been so peaceful here, and now you are back ranting and raving." She rang the bell and when Humphrey answered it, Lucinda ordered brandy.

"At least you have the decency to see to my wants," the marquess said sarcastically.

"Did you want brandy as well? I ordered it for myself."

Before the marquess could say anything, Humphrey appeared with the brandy. The marquess was in such a rage, he did not realize it was very odd for the brandy to make its appearance so quickly, not knowing Lucinda had warned Humphrey to have a decanter and two glasses ready in the hall should her husband be waiting for her when she returned home.

Humphrey poured out two glasses, bowed, and left. Lucinda fished in her reticule and took out a flat case. She extracted a cheroot, heaved herself out of the chair, took a taper from its pot by the fire, and lit the cheroot. Then she picked up her glass of brandy, winked vulgarly at the marquess, and said, "No heel taps."

The marquess snatched the cheroot out of her hand and threw it in the fire. Lucinda reached over and grabbed his brandy glass and threw that in the fire as well. There was an explosion as the spirit hit the flames, followed by a sinister rumbling from the chimney.

"I knew I had forgotten something," Lucinda said. "I forgot to have the chimneys swept.

The rumbling grew louder. Lucinda ran to the door. "No you don't," yelled the marquess, seizing her around the waist. "If you behave like a doxy, you will be treated like a doxy."

There was a great *whump* from behind him as a huge pile of soot landed on the hearth. Then it spread out over the room, turning everything black.

"Now, my wife," said the marquess, oblivious of the fact that he and Lucinda were now as black as chimney sweeps. He forced his mouth down on her own. Lucinda groped desperately at a brooch on her dress, got it unfastened, and stabbed him in the arm.

He let out a cry and released her.

Lucinda looked at the marquess. His face was completely black except for his lips. She began to giggle. "You do look silly, Rockingham," she said, and then she turned and ran from the room.

The marquess could never in all his life remember being so angry. He walked to the desk, took out a pistol and primed it, and then mounted the stairs.

Lucinda heard him coming but she was not afraid. Encouraged by Mr. Dancer, she had drunk a great deal of wine at the supper which followed the opera. There was nothing Rockingham could do. The door was firmly locked.

And then there came a deafening explosion as the marquess shot the lock away.

But Lucinda had had a bolt put on the door as well.

The marquess kicked in the door, sending splinters flying everywhere.

He grabbed Lucinda by the hair and began to kiss her, savagely and passionately and without one single scrap of love or affection.

Lucinda fought desperately. Several times she managed to tear herself out of his embrace, but before she could reach the door, he dragged her back again.

Finally he threw her on the bed and pinned her beneath him. "Now," he said, "we shall taste some of the favors you have been giving Dancer."

Beaten and frightened, Lucinda lay still in his arms while the tears began to course down her cheeks.

The marquess felt the wetness against his own cheeks and raised his head and looked down at her, more shocked than he would have been had she struck him.

"No, not like this, Lucinda," he whispered. "What a mess you are! All black face and white tear marks. Hush, love, I have a filthy temper. You must not cry."

"You are horrible . . . horrible . . . a beast!" she sobbed.

"I know. Hush now. It is all right. I shall not take you by force. Hush."

He rocked her in his arms until her sobs died away. Then she lay quietly in his arms, looking in wonder at his altered face. "Your wild ways frighten me, Rockingham," she said at last.

"I have a devil of a temper. When did you start drinking brandy and smoking cheroots?"

"Only this evening," said Lucinda. "I wanted you to get a taste of your own medicine. If you can sleep with Maria Deauville, drink to excess, and smoke cheroots, then why can't I behave just as badly?"

"How did you find out about Maria?"

"It was not difficult. Ismene told me the gossip the first day I arrived in London. And the lady herself told me she had been in Paris with you."

"I left the minute she arrived. There are no women in my life, Lucinda."

"How can I believe that?"

"A little patience, a little trust. What of you and Dancer?"

"He was friendly. I was lonely. I don't know. But I have not been unfaithful to you. You should know I could not do that."

"No, perhaps not. But women are cruel and changeable."

"Perhaps the women you have known. Why do you behave so badly?"

"Boredom. Besides, it always annoyed my parents, and from an early age, I would do anything to annoy them."

"That is dreadful. One must honor one's father and mother."

"You have met my mother, have you not?"

"Yes. But . . . I do not know much of the world. My own mother was loving and kind, my father also."

"My parents were monsters of cruelty. They did not discipline me, they tortured me. I grew up cold and cynical. I trust no one, except perhaps Chumley."

"And yet you expect my trust?"

The marquess dropped a light kiss on her sooty nose. "I demand so much and yet know so little of you, madam wife."

She was still pressed closely against him and her body began to burn and throb. She could almost feel her lips swellling as they ached for his kiss. She could not understand it. Her mind was telling her he was dangerous and not to be provoked but her wanton body was sending out shameful messages. She hoped he would not notice.

But the glow in the strange green eyes so near to her own told her he *had* noticed. He bent his head and softly kissed her eyelids, and then his mouth moved to the nape of her neck.

"Don't," she whispered weakly. "It is too soon." She tried to conjure up Mr. Dancer's face, but found she could not even remember what he looked like. Her husband's hands were stroking her body and making every part of it strain toward him.

His exploring mouth moved to the tops of her breasts and then nuzzled the material down, searching further. "Please stop," said Lucinda. "Oh, please," she moaned.

He raised his hand and looked at her with a touch of arrogance. "You will need to be my wife in more than name soon enough."

"But not yet," she said, closing her eyes. "Not like this. Not without love."

In the next minute he was off the bed and out of the room, slamming what was left of the door behind him.

Lucinda spent a long time the following morning trying on one gown after another. She felt a need to be armored in the best fashion before confronting her erratic husband at the breakfast table. At last, wearing a gown of pale green muslin with little puffed sleeves and a demure neckline, and with her longer hair piled up on top of her head, she went into the breakfast room.

The marquess was sitting reading the newspaper. He glanced up in an abstracted way as she came in, and then continued reading. Humphrey presented Lucinda with her usual breakfast of tea and toast and then retired. Silence fell on the room, apart from the mournful ticking of the Iphigenia clock and the hissing of the urn.

The marquess was looking very handsome. He was wrapped in a gaudy Oriental dressing gown and his fine cambric shirt was open at the neck, showing the strong column of his throat. His black hair had grown quite long.

"Good morning," Lucinda said loudly.

Again the green eyes glanced at her with an indifferent look before the marquess hid himself behind the newspaper again.

Lucinda's wayward body screamed for

kisses and caresses. He had kissed her intimately, she thought, turning scarlet as she remembered the feel of his lips on her breast, and yet it meant nothing to him.

"Your hair is too long," she said in a voice which sounded shrill in her own ears. He put down the paper.

"What did you say?"

"Your hair is too long, Rockingham. You look ridiculous. You look like one of the minor prophets."

The marquess felt a stab of hurt. He was amazed at that feeling of hurt, but did not spend any time examining it.

"You are hardly in a position to criticize anyone's appearance."

"What is up with my appearance?"

"For a start," the marquess said nastily, "your mouth is much too big."

"It is not!"

"Yes, it is. Enormous. Ear to ear, I assure you."

Lucinda seized the tea urn and tried to throw it. It was too heavy but it toppled across the table. The marquess leapt out of the road as a waterfall of scalding tea rushed toward him.

"You silly jade. Have you no consideration for the servants who will have to clean this mess?"

"*You* talk to me about consideration for the servants! May I remind you, my lord, you could never keep a servant. Or have you forgot? Of course you have. You are so drunk most of the time you cannot remember a thing."

"I remember kissing you," he said softly.

"Ooooh!" screamed Lucinda. "I *hate* you!"

She ran from the room and up the stairs. But once in the sanctuary of her own room and after a hearty bout of tears, she began to wonder whether she were mad. She had not planned to behave so dreadfully at breakfast. But his indifference had hurt. And her mouth was *not* too big. She ran to the mirror and stared at it miserably, trying by primming up her lips to reduce its generous size.

Lucinda picked up a book, determined to stay in her room until he left the house. The print danced before her angry hurt eyes and she found she was reading the same sentence over and over again. Then at last she heard him mounting the stairs and his voice calling loudly for Chumley. She waited, sure he would come to her. After half an hour, she heard his footsteps going down the stairs and then the opening of the front door. She ran to the window and looked down.

One of the new grooms had brought around the marquess's phaeton. The marquess said something to the groom, who smiled and touched his jockey cap. How these servants of mine fawn over him, Lucinda thought. Before I came, he could not even *keep* a groom!

The marquess leapt into his carriage and picked up the reins. Then around the square came another phaeton, driving by Maria Deauville. Jealousy like poison swept through Lucinda's body as she noticed how competently pretty little Mrs. Deauville handled the reins. She saw her husband stiffen. His hands dropped the reins.

Maria cast a quick look up at the house and saw Lucinda watching, but so quick was that glance that Lucinda did not know she had been seen. Her husband's head was turned away from her so that she could not see his expression, but she could see Maria's.

Her face glowed; her glance was caressing. She leaned across her carriage and whispered something to the marquess, who gave an abrupt nod, picked up the reins, and drove off.

She has made an assignation, Lucinda thought bitterly.

Once more, Mr. Dancer's handsome face came back into her mind. Now, there was a man who loved her, who would cherish her.

Undecided as to what to do to ease the pain at her heart, she prepared to go out.

As she was putting on her bonnet,

Humphrey came in to say that Mr. Carter had called.

"Tell him I cannot see him," said Lucinda crossly.

"But, my lady," said Humphrey, "Mr. Carter says it is not a social call. He has called in reply to your advertisement about Kennedy in the *Morning Post!*"

11

Mr. Carter had been frightened to death when he had seen that advertisement. Benson had disappeared, never to be heard of again. Now it appeared Kennedy, the maid Benson had used to elicit information, had disappeared as well.

He was suddenly sure Maria had finally run mad and killed them both, or had them killed. He knew Maria often took more opium than was good for her. The drug must have turned her brain. Now Rockingham, surely, must know of his wife's concern for the missing maid, and Rockingham would get to the bottom of it. If he accused Maria, then Maria would bring him, Zeus Carter, down with her.

In his ears, Mr. Carter could swear he heard the tolling of the great bell of St. Sepulchre's and in his mind's eye, he could see himself mounting the scaffold outside Newgate, looking down into the avid, greedy faces of the watching mob. Maria and her friends, he knew, enjoyed a public hanging as much as they enjoyed the playhouse. Mr. Carter had accompanied them once and had disgraced himself by being violently sick.

He waited in Berkeley Square until he saw Rockingham leave. The sight of Maria driving up caused Mr. Carter to whimper with terror and dive behind a tree for shelter.

He waited and waited until he was sure there was no sign of either his cousin or Maria Deauville returning to the square. Feeling breathless and sick, he called on Lucinda.

Mr. Carter felt Lucinda was growing more like a haughty marchioness every day. Her height lent her dignity and there was a cold, arrogant look in her eyes as she stared down at him. She did not ask him to be seated, but in icy tones demanded the reason for his visit.

"I saw your advertisement, ma'am," said Mr. Carter. " 'Pon rep. I was struck all of a heap."

There was a silence while Mr. Carter pulled out a little fan and fanned himself vigorously. Lucinda said impatiently, "If you know something about Kennedy, pray tell me."

Mr. Carter looked at her pleadingly. He tried to think of some light and airy way to phrase it; some way to cover up the intense dread he felt. But he blurted out, "I saw Kennedy, your maid, often in the company of

Benson, Maria Deauville's lady's maid—a servant who has also gone missing."

"I cannot believe Kennedy would have gone off with someone—no matter how great a friend—without telling me. Since Mrs. Deauville is a friend of yours, did you not ask her what had happened to *her* maid?"

"Not a friend of mine. Not *at all!* I did ask and she said that Benson—let me see how she put it—she said, 'Benson is, or was, my maid.' "

"No further explanation?"

"To be frank with you, I found I dared not ask."

Lucinda frowned. "What would Kennedy be about, to strike up a friendship with the maid of a woman who has shown she dislikes me and is jealous of me?"

"Perhaps Kennedy did not know that Benson was maid to Maria Deauville, or perhaps it could be the name meant nothing to her and she imagined Mrs. Deauville to be a respectable lady with no, um, connection with your family."

Lucinda looked down at him sharply. "You appear remarkably acute at guessing what Kennedy might or might not think. *I* am beginning to think that perhaps Benson was sent to befriend Kennedy and therefore spy on me." Lucinda suddenly blushed with mortification. The horrible Maria would know of the lock on the bedroom door, of the scenes.

"I cannot tell you more," cried Mr. Carter, backing away. "The reward you promised in your advertisement . . . ?"

"As you know, I have no money of my own, and such money as I do have is Rockingham's. I shall tell him of your visit and no doubt he will call to see you."

"No, no. Pray do not tell him. Forget the reward."

"But, as I remember," Lucinda said, advancing on him, "you are Rockingham's cousin and boon companion."

"I lied," squeaked Mr. Carter. "Rockingham despises me." He burst into noisy tears and ran from the room.

Rockingham should be here to help me with this, thought Lucinda. But he is no doubt safely in the arms of his scheming mistress. Bah! There is one who would aid me.

She called a footman and sent him with a note to Mr. Dancer's lodgings and then sat down to wait.

Mr. Dancer came very promptly, since Lucinda had had the foresight to put in her note that Rockingham was not at home.

When Lucinda had explained the problem, Mr. Dancer's eyes narrowed. He did not want

Maria to be found guilty of anything or she might turn on him and tell Lucinda about the plot to ruin her. He decided to help Lucinda track down her maid and see if he could find some opportunity during the day to press his suit. Maria's reward was no longer the incentive. Mr. Dancer was convinced he loved Lucinda to distraction.

He told her that he had seen Maria in Oxford Street. Since she was gone from home, he would take the opportunity of calling at Manchester Square and questioning her servants. He promised to return as soon as possible.

He was absent only a half-hour. On his return, he said that on the night Benson had disappeared, Maria had driven off with her to an inn somewhere off the Richmond road. Find what happened to Benson, said Mr. Dancer eagerly, and then you will find what happened to Kennedy. He had obtained the name of the inn from one of Maria's grooms. Furthermore, Quinton, Maria's butler, had said that Kennedy had called to try to find out what had become of Benson and had looked most upset.

"And what is the name of this inn?" asked Lucinda.

"The Red Lion, near Syon Park. Allow me to take you there."

Mr. Dancer hoped to have a chance of awakening some reciprocal passion in Lucinda's bosom before the expedition was over.

"Very well. I shall go and put on my cloak, for the day has turned cold."

Lucinda was about to leave her bedchamber when she turned back. She should not really be driving anywhere with Mr. Dancer. Trying to revenge herself on her faithless husband by appearing to behave the same way did not give her any satisfaction. On the other hand, she was determined to solve the mystery of Kennedy's disappearance.

She sat down at a little desk in the corner and wrote a note of explanation, saying that as she badly needed help to be driven to the Red Lion near Richmond in order to find out what had become of Kennedy and because he, Rockingham, was no doubt *otherwise engaged*, she had called on the services of Mr. Dancer. She sanded the letter, rang the bell, and told Humphrey to give it to the marquess when he returned.

As they drove out of London, Mr. Dancer reflected that had Maria been stupid enough to murder her maid, then she would surely have covered her tracks. He expected the investigation to come to a dead end. The inn sounded secluded. Perhaps a good place to woo Lucinda.

The day was humid with a busy, bustling wind. Dust from the road blew into Lucinda's face and she wished she had brought a veil and defied the fashion critics who damned veils as vulgar.

Lucinda kept thinking about her husband and Maria, and the more she thought about it, the more wretched and miserable she became. Long before they reached the inn, Lucinda had decided to ask the marquess for her freedom. She cast a sidelong look at Mr. Dancer. He appeared as handsome and pleasant as ever. And yet Lucinda felt there was something vaguely sinister about him. Against the backdrop of the West End of London, he looked very urbane and sophisticated, one of many fashionable men. Now, against a view of summer fields and grazing cattle with great puffy clouds like galleons being tugged across the sky above on a high wind, he looked out of place, wrong . . . false.

All Lucinda decided she wanted to do was to find out what had become of Kennedy and then return to her father away from this bewildering world of vicious, idle people.

Having reminded herself that all she had to do was to flee from both her husband and Mr. Dancer as soon as possible, Lucinda felt more composed as the carriage swept into the inn courtyard.

* * *

The Marquess of Rockingham stood at the counter of Rundell and Bridge's turning necklace after necklace over in his fingers, holding first one and then another up to the light. After Maria had whispered to him in the square that she bore him no ill will and wished him well in his marriage, the marquess—not knowing that Maria had said the first thing that came into her head because she knew Lucinda was watching and wanted to create a picture of intimacy—felt like celebrating. He had anticipated a scene. To his surprise, he found his ideas of celebrating seemed to have changed. He wanted to buy his wife a present.

Everything about Lucinda hit him in a sort of rush—her spirit, her gallantry, her courage, her elusive charm. He began to feel light-headed, almost as if he *had* been drinking.

He could not remember her wearing any jewelry at all. So he stood in London's most famous jeweler's, looking carefully at necklaces, determined to buy the most beautiful one in the shop. Diamonds were out of fashion. Semiprecious stones were all the rage. And yet there was one magnificent necklace the marquess found he favored above the rest. It was made of huge rubies set in old gold. It was heavy, almost barbaric, but the stones were magnificent, burning in the gloom of the shop with a red fire of their own.

"Buying another bauble for one of your mistresses?" came a voice from behind him.

The marquess turned slowly around and found himself facing his mother. He turned back. "I shall take this one," he said, stuffing it in his pocket. "Send me the bill."

Without another look at the duchess, he opened the shop door and went out into the noise and racket of Ludgate Hill.

The old restless feeling came back and with it all the old misery. But the weight of the necklace dragging at his pocket was a comfort. A smile curved his lips. Would his incalculable wife accept it with grace or throw it in his face?

He sprang into his carriage and set out for home, looking forward to seeing Lucinda's face when he gave her the present.

The inn was deserted. Sounds came from abovestairs. Mr. Dancer saw the green of the garden at the back and suggested to Lucinda that they wait out in the fresh air until the landlord appeared.

The table Maria had had shifted about was still placed at the edge of the pond. Mr. Dancer thought it looked a romantic spot. He would wait until she had asked her tiresome questions and then he would get down on one knee—he hoped the grass was not damp—and swear everlasting love.

The landlord came into the garden. "Good afternoon," he said, bowing low. "I thought I heard someone arrive. What is your pleasure?"

"Let us order some wine first," urged Mr. Dancer, "and you may question this fellow when he returns." Lucinda said she would prefer lemonade. Mr. Dancer ordered a bottle of burgundy. The landlord bowed and left them alone.

The irritating, gusty wind had died down and a mellow golden light bathed the pond and garden. A blackbird sang with aching sweetness from the branch of a lilac tree. Lucinda's eyes filled with tears.

Mr. Dancer seized her hand. "My lady, your distress cuts me to the quick. Pray forget about this folly of looking for a tiresome servant, and—"

But Lucinda snatched her hand away. "I am in no mood for dalliance," she said. "I wish you had let me question the landlord right away."

"I think that you forget I love you passionately," said Mr. Dancer in a low voice.

"Please do not go in this strain," said Lucinda. "*You* forget, I am married."

"And yet, in your trouble, you sent for me."

Lucinda bit her lip. Oh, if only she could return to town, tell her husband she was leaving him, and retire back to the country and forget about Kennedy! But she must try to find out what had become of her lady's maid. Mr. Dancer's beautiful blue eyes were surveying her sympathetically, and yet for the first time Lucinda seemed to catch a glimpse of something lurking in the brilliant blue depths, something predatory. For the first time, she began to feel a little afraid of Mr. Dancer.

"I should not have traveled with you," Lucinda said. "Mr. Dancer, I fear I can never return your love."

There came a chinking of bottles against glasses from the direction of the inn. Mr. Dancer muttered something under his breath.

It was not the landlord who was approaching the table, but a tall, angular woman in cap and apron. No doubt the landlord's wife, he thought.

Then he realized Lucinda was staring at this female, her face white.

The maid put the bottles and glasses on the table and curtsied. "Can I fetch you anything, sir, madam?"

"Kennedy," whispered Lucinda. "It's Kennedy!"

The maid looked at Lucinda with a puzzled expression in her eyes. "Beg pardon, mum?"

"Kennedy, do you not know me? It is I, Lucinda, Marchioness of Rockingham."

Kennedy put a work-worn hand up to her brow. "Silas," she called suddenly. "Silas, come quick!"

The landlord came running out of the inn. "What have you been doing to upset Jane?" he demanded.

"But this is Kennedy, Amy Kennedy, my maid," said Lucinda.

"My love," said Mr. Dancer smoothly, "it is obvious you have made a mistake."

"No," said Lucinda stubbornly. "She must have lost her memory."

"Well, that may be the case," said the landlord. "I am Silas Snodgrass. This woman I call Jane came wandering into the inn one night—'twas the night of that fearsome storm. She was soaked through and had a huge lump on the back of her head like she'd been struck by something, and she didn't know who she was or where she came from. I'm a widower, see, and I need a housekeeper here bad. So after she recovered her health, I asked her to stay on so's she could earn her keep till her memory come back. We suit very well, me and Jane, and fact is, we was going to get spliced come next Martinmas."

Kennedy looked at Lucinda. "I do know you, my lady, and yet I don't, if you take my meaning."

"Kennedy," said Lucinda gently, "you evidently came to this inn to look for a friend of yours, a maid who had also disappeared. She was called Benson."

But Kennedy was hardly listening. "If I am who you say I am, my lady, you must not order me back, for I am mortal fond of Silas here."

"No, no, Kennedy. You may stay. I have no hold over you. But listen again. Benson. A maid called Benson. Maid to a Mrs. Maria Deauville. She came here with her mistress and was never seen again."

Kennedy wearily shook her head.

"When would that be, my lady?" put in the landlord. "For a lady come here the night of the storm and gave a note to my stableboy to give to another lady what come in a post chaise. He's shortsighted and didn't get a good look at either of them."

"No, it was before then," said Lucinda. "I cannot give you a description of Benson—"

"Ah, but I can!" cried Mr. Dancer. "She is of middle-age, thin and wiry, with dark hair streaked with gray."

The landlord looked puzzled.

"Her mistress, then," said Mr. Dancer. "An exquisite creature dressed always in the first stare with golden hair and blue eyes, very beautiful and very dainty."

"Ah, her," said the landlord, his face

clearing. "I mind her. And you're right. She had a maid with her just like what you described. Let me see. She messed about a bit, getting me to move tables here and there in the garden. Why! She was setting right here. Right at the edge of the pond. Now, she ordered two glasses of ratafee. I could not see her from the windows, for you'll see this table is out of sight of them. Her maid comes back through the inn and says to me not to bother them till I'm summoned. She was going out to the carriage to fetch something. Now, I swore I caught a glimpse of her coming back, but the carter arrived and I went out to see him.

"Then the lady comes into the inn and pays her shot and asks for her maid. I says I haven't seen her and she says, oh, she must be in the carriage. That's all I know."

There was a long silence and then slowly everyone's eyes turned in the direction of the pond.

"No, I cannot believe it, even of her," said Lucinda.

"You are quite right. What you are thinking is ridiculous." Mr. Dancer laughed. "How gothic."

"If only Kennedy could remember something," said Lucinda.

"I've got an old boat hook out back," said Silas Snodgrass. "I'll fetch it direct and fish around the pond a bit."

"No!" cried Mr. Dancer, but the landlord was already making his way rapidly toward the inn. There came the sound of a carriage arriving. Kennedy bobbed a curtsy. "I'll just attend to whoever has arrived, my lady," she said, "and then I will come straight back."

If Maria had been stupid enough to kill her maid and dump the body in the pond, thought Mr. Dancer desperately, then Kennedy, who might regain her memory, would be taken back to London to accuse Maria. Mr. Dancer was sure from the landlord's tale that of the two women who had visited the inn during the storm, one of them had been Maria and the other Kennedy. Maria probably thought she had killed Kennedy. Perhaps she had struck her and left her for dead.

His frightened thoughts swung back to Lucinda. If he could get Lucinda to run away with him, then he could take her out of London.

"Lucinda," he said. He stood up and walked around the table. Lucinda stood up as well. He pulled her into his arms and smiled into her eyes. "Forget this nonsense," he whispered. "Come away with me. I will keep you safe from Rockingham until your marriage is annulled."

"It is not so easy to get a marriage annulled," Lucinda said, pushing him away.

"It is easy . . . if the marraige has not been consummated, as yours has not."

Lucinda backed away, her eyes wide with shock. "You know," she said. "it is all a plot. Benson sent to spy on Kennedy, Benson gossiping to Mrs. Deauville, Mrs. Deauville plotting with you to ruin me."

She made to run toward the inn, but he caught her arm.

And then the Marquess of Rockingham charged into the garden. With a roar of fury, he rushed at Mr. Dancer, picked him up as if he weighed no more than a child, and threw him into the pond. Kennedy and Silas came running out.

"Come out so I can hit you again!" shouted the marquess, standing with his hands on his hips at the water's edge.

Mr. Dancer crawled to the edge. "I was escorting your wife at her request," he said miserably. "I . . ."

Then his face took on a greenish pallor and he stood up. "There is something rotten here," he whispered.

He had trodden on Benson's body, which lay at the bottom of the pond. His foot had struck the rotting canvas money belt and the threads had finally parted. What was left of Benson's body slowly rose to the surface.

12

HALF-DRUGGED WITH OPIUM, Maria Deauville stretched lazily in bed. She glanced at the clock and judged she had at least another hour before rising to begin making preparations for the evening ahead.

Opposite the bed hung a portrait of her late husband, Henri Deauville, a French émigré, who still had had most of the fortune he had taken out of France just before the Terror, when he had met Maria. He had been considerably older than she and had not lived long after the marriage. Maria never thought about him much and, even at the best of times, she had only a hazy memory of what he had been like. She had a capacity for living in the minute and never agonized very much about what she had done the year before or even the day before.

Vain and self-centered, nonetheless she had permitted the Marquess of Rockingham to become the only man ever to touch her heart. She reveled in his rakishness, feeling they were both of a kind. But most men, Maria knew, however rakish, could be depended on to settle down at last, and she had had every hope that when the marquess at last decided to marry, he would choose her.

Her eyes suddenly opened wide at the sound of the commotion in the street below. She rose groggily from her bed and pulled on a wrapper. She tugged aside the curtains and looked down into Montague Street. The first thing she saw was Mr. Carter standing on the other side. His face was so white, his gaze so agonized as he stared at her house, that she threw up the window, leaned out, and looked down.

One glance was enough.

She drew her head in quickly, her heart beating hard.

Down below was a line of carriages. On the pavement stood Rockingham, Lucinda, two Bow Street Runners, a man who looked like a magistrate . . . and Kennedy.

Her hand went to the bell to ring for Quinton and tell him to bar the door, and then fell to her side. Quinton would not refuse admittance to the Runners.

She slung a mantle around her shoulders and then rushed to her jewel box and began to stuff jewels into her pockets and fastened several necklaces about her neck. She clasped bracelets of precious stones about her wrists.

Putting on a pair of flat shoes, she paused only a moment to listen to the thunderous knocking on the door below.

She ran from her bedroom and began to climb up the stairs to the attics, where she knew there was a ladder leading to the roof.

Below her came the thud of footsteps running up the stairs. Once out on the roof, she slithered down the tiles to the parapet and then started inching her way along. Maria meant to try to make her escape along the roofs. But the effects of the opium she had taken made her dizzy. Below her the street reeled and danced. A crowd was collecting, pointing upward, all staring at the fantastic figure of Maria, bedecked with glittering jewels, her cloak open over her nightdress, swaying in the sunlight.

She had locked the skylight behind her, but with a crash, the lock was shattered and the Marquess of Rockingham climbed through. He, too, slid down to the parapet, then stood upright and advanced on her.

"You murderess," he said.

"I did it for you, Rockingham," pleaded Maria. "All for you. You should have married me. I love you."

"No," said the marquess, horrified. "I will

take no blame for the brutal murder of your poor maid."

"Let me escape," pleaded Maria. "Please, Rockingham."

"You did not let Benson escape," he said. "And you thought you had killed Kennedy. You must stand trial."

Maria closed her eyes for a moment. She had attended so many public hangings that she knew what it would be like to be the chief performer.

"Please . . ." she whispered again.

At that moment a Runner poked his head through the skylight and leveled a pistol at Maria. "Stay where you are," he ordered. "In the king's name, I—"

But that was as far as he got.

With a loud scream, Maria Deauville jumped.

The marquess crouched down and leaned over the edge. Maria lay in the middle of the road, her head at an awkward angle.

Jewels lay spilled about her.

There was a great roar from the people in the street.

The marquess closed his eyes as the greedy crowd closed in on the body, grabbing and tearing at the jewels.

Mr. Zeus Carter went straight to Mr.

Dancer's lodgings, to find that gentleman supervising the packing of his trunks.

"Maria has killed herself," said Mr. Carter. "Oh, my heart! Jumped to her death. From the roof of her own house! Rockingham and the Runners were there."

"Take those cases down to the carriage," Mr. Dancer ordered his servants. Then he turned to Mr. Carter and said harshly, "Did she talk before she died?"

"I do not know," said Mr. Carter, beginning to cry. "Rockingham was with her on the roof. Where are you going?"

"I am going to Paris in case Maria has told Rockingham of the plot to ruin his wife."

"Take me with you," begged Mr. Carter. "He will kill me."

"I am not waiting in town for you to pack!"

Mr. Carter began to cry harder than ever.

"Oh, the deuce. Go and fetch your traps and meet me at the Wheatsheaf on the Dover Road. Do you know it?"

Mr. Carter nodded, and gulped.

"Then be off with you, or Rockingham will eat us both for his dinner!"

The two were eventually fortunate in their escape. For by the time the marquess had completed all the statements necessary about Maria Deauville's guilt and manner of death, the couple were well on their way.

The marquess returned home after having failed to find either of them. He remembered the elation he had felt when he had bought that necklace for Lucinda. Now he felt miserable and guilty. To have had a mistress before marriage was just about as common in society as it was to have a mistress after marriage. But to have kept a mistress who was a murderess! How could he explain that? How could he explain that his relations with his mother had colored his view of women? That he had never in his life contemplated being married to anyone who would have any emotional hold on him whatsoever? His conscience told him he could at least start off by apologizing, but his conscience was at war with all his aristocratic upbringing. Gentlemen never apologized.

He pushed down the door of his home in Berkeley Square, to be met by those now-familiar smells of flowers and beeswax and applewood fires.

But there was an empty air about the place. The very spirit of home had fled.

So he was not surprised when Chumley with a face like a fiddle handed him a letter from his wife.

He went into the saloon and slumped down in a chair and looked at it a long time without opening it.

At last he broke the seal.

"Dear Rockingham," he read, "I am gone to Lord Chamfreys' to join my father. I think you must understand that after today's events I am come to my senses and must demand an annulment of our marriage. Nonetheless, I remain deeply grateful to you for rescuing me from Lady Ismene. You must see, however, that we could never suit. I remain, Yr. obedient servant, L."

He put down the letter on his lap and stared miserably at the dancing flames of the fire. Most of society stopped lighting fires at the end of March and did not think it necessary to warm their houses until the beginning of September. Only such a homemaker as Lucinda appreciated that the English climate was never really warm.

Chumley stood outside the door, waiting for the shout to get the carriage ready. Another night's wild dissipation would be in the cards, of that he was sure.

When the expected shout came, he went sadly into the saloon.

But the marquess's words surprised him. "Chumley, why the deuce has my lady gone to Chamfreys'? Does she not know her father is at Cramley, looking after the alterations to the gardens?"

"No, my lord," said Chumley. "My lady

simply said to me she was going to join her father. I naturally assumed you would have told her all about removing Mr. Westerville to Cramley."

"Order the carriage, Chumley," said the marquess, "and pack my things."

"Yes, my lord," said Chumley, his face breaking into a rare smile. "Right away, my lord."

"Which carriage did my lady take?"

"She went post chaise, my lord."

"Good, then perhaps we can catch up with her. She will need to put up somewhere on the road for the night."

At the Pelican posting house, Lucinda prepared wearily to go downstairs to the dining room for a late supper. Her mind told her she had had a lucky escape from such as the marquess. Her heart ached with longing. It was going to be hard to get over a man who did not even love her. She could not understand her own distress. Rockingham was a brute and a rake.

She entered the dining room. The only other occupants were a clergyman and his wife and two small children. Lucinda nodded politely to them and sat down, feeling she should eat something, but longing only for sleep and the oblivion it would bring.

To the landlord's disappointment, my lady turned down all his exotic dishes and said she merely wanted some bread and water and a cold collation.

She was dismally pushing the meat on her plate around with her fork when the door of the dining room crashed open. The clergyman's wife let out a squeak of fright and Lucinda looked up.

Her husband was standing on the threshold, still attired in the black coat, buckskin breeches, and top boots he had worn during the day.

He came over to her table and sat down opposite her.

"You should have had the decency to spare me any scenes, Rockingham," Lucinda said in a low voice.

"I am come, lady," said the marquess in a level voice, "to tell you you are going in the wrong direction. Mr. Westerville is at Cramley."

"Your home! Why?"

"I removed him from Chamfreys' because he had recovered. When I was at Cramley, I started alterations to my gardens. I needed someone to supervise the work. My father-in-law, I decided, would be better helping me than slaving for an ungrateful vicar."

"You did that?"

"I am not entirely a monster," he said with a rueful smile.

"But," said Lucinda, dropping her voice to a whisper, "you did have a mistress in keeping —a mistress who was a murderess."

"And you, Miss Prim and Proper, thought nothing of traveling into the country with London's most notorious seducer."

"That was different. Mr. Dancer hasn't killed anyone."

"As far as you know," the marquess said cynically.

"Rockingham. It is of no use. Nothing will mend this marriage. I must see my father. All I want is to return to the simplicity of my old life. We shall contrive somehow, and have no right to be your pensioners."

"We must discuss this further."

Lucinda wearily pushed her plate away and got to her feet. "Not this evening. I am exhausted."

She curtsied and left the dining room. The landlord appeared after she had gone and the marquess ordered food and then sat pushing it around his plate much as his wife had done.

When Lucinda reached her room, she found a connecting door to the next room was now unlocked and standing open. She marched into the next room and found Chumley in the process of unpacking his master's clothes.

"Chumley," Lucinda said severely, "I want this door locked and bolted."

"Very good, my lady."

Lucinda waited in her own room with her arms folded until she heard the key click in the lock, and then she began to prepare for bed.

She was just slipping her nightgown over her head when she heard her husband's voice from behind the connecting door.

"Lucinda! May I come in? I have something for you."

"No!" she called, thinking it was maddening that the lock and key should be on his side and therefore she had wasted her time in getting Chumley to secure it. "I am going to sleep."

But she heard the key turn in the lock and her husband walked in.

He fished in the pocket of the tails of his coat and pulled out the necklace and threw it on the bed.

"I bought this for you," he said, not looking at her. "You may as well have it."

Lucinda picked up the heavy gold-and-ruby necklace. "It is beautiful, Rockingham," she said with a catch in her voice. "But I fear I have no longer any right to take it."

"Oh, take the bauble," he said furiously,

remembering with misery all the love he had felt for her when he had bought it.

He turned away.

Something made Lucinda ask, "Why did you buy it?"

"Because you are my marchioness, and I noticed you did not have any jewelry," he said impatiently. He stood looking at her, haughtily, arrogantly, and then he added, "And because I am in love with you, dammit!"

Her eyes were very large and dark in the candlelight and her thick hair was now long enough to curl on her shoulders. "I have never had a more beautiful present in my life, Rockingham."

"I am glad it pleases you," he replied curtly.

"I am not talking about the necklace," Lucinda said. "I am talking about your words. Do you really love me?"

All the hauteur and arrogance and pride fell from the marquess. "I suppose so," he mumbed. "Now, if you will excuse me, madam—"

"Oh, Rockingham," Lucinda cried, throwing herself into his arms. "Why did you not say so before? I have been so unhappy."

"How am I supposed to recognize love easily when it comes?" he said huskily. "It is all so new to me. It took me some time to know what I felt for you."

"I thought all you felt for me was a mixture of anger and lust."

He silenced her with a kiss—a kiss that went on and on, a kiss that started as one of chaste tenderness and respect and ended up a hot fusing of mounting passions.

Next door, Chumley stood holding his master's nightgown and cap. He heard a tremendous crash from next door and raised his eyes to heaven.

"You knocked over the water jug," Lucinda said. "Look, there is water all over the floor."

"I was trying to carry you to bed," her husband grumbled.

"You are determined not to wait until the six months is up," she said.

He put her down gently on the bed and lay next to her. "I shall wait . . . if you wish it."

"Perhaps. I am afraid."

"Don't be," he said, drawing her into his arms.

"Oh, Rockingham, you have got your boots on."

"My name is Julian. And I am about to remove my boots."

"What if I cry 'Stop?' You will be so furious with me."

"I'll try not to be, my love," he said, sending one boot flying, and then the other.

Behind the door, Chumley brightened. At

least he had taken off his boots. Was there *hope?*

"Now, my sweeting," the marquess said at *last.* "No boots, no clothes, only me. Kiss me, Lucinda."

About the Author

Born in Glasgow, Scotland, Ms. Chesney started her writing career while working as a fiction buyer in a bookstore in Glasgow. She doubled as a theater critic, newspaper reporter, and editor before coming to the United States in 1971. She later returned to London, where she lives with her husband and one child near Kensington Palace.